THE DERBY MAN TRAPPED

High above the freezing spray of the American River, supported only by a reed work basket . . .

The fuses caught instantly and spluttered with smoke and white-hot light. When the fifth one took off, Darby yelled, "Take us up!"

As if in response, a heavy caliber rifle thundered over the river and its big slug tore straight up, ripping through the basket's floor.

"Look out!" Darby shouted.

Like a fist, the next slug of the ambusher's weapon punched up between Darby's legs and tore a ragged gash of flesh and reed across the inside of Darby's calf before it hummed meanly away.

"Take us up!" he roared.

But, even as he felt the rope jerk, he knew it was too late. In one awful second, they'd either get shot, blasted off the cliff face by the five sizzling fuses, or the miserable reeds underfoot were going to separate enough to open like a death funnel.

The Derby Man gnashed his teeth—they didn't have a Chinaman's chance.

— For Jim —

EXPLOSION
AT
DONNER PASS

Gary McCarthy

Really enjoyed

talking to you
at dinner. Hope
you enjoy this one.
Sincerely,
Gary McCarthy

EXPLOSION AT DONNER PASS
A Bantam Book / June 1981

ISBN 0–553–14745–5

Published simultaneously in the United States and Canada

Bantam Books are published by Bantam Books, Inc. Its trademark, consisting of the words "Bantam Books" and the por-
trayal of a bantam, is Registered in U.S. Patent and Trademark
Office and in other countries. Marca Registrada. Bantam
Books, Inc., 666 Fifth Avenue, New York, New York 10103.

PRINTED IN THE UNITED STATES OF AMERICA

0 9 8 7 6 5 4 3 2 1

For Lonnie Beesley, at heart, a railroad man.

EXPLOSION
AT
DONNER PASS

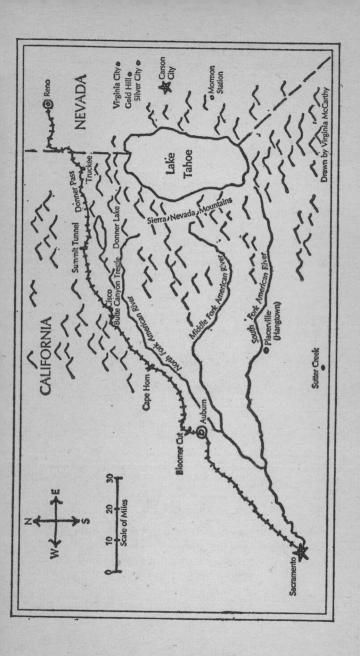

Chapter 1

Darby Buckingham gazed across the candlelit table into the limpid, azure depths of his woman's eyes. This evening marked the third anniversary of their unforgettable meeting in Running Springs, Wyoming. And, since it was so special, and because they both loved to eat, they'd celebrated by ordering the most sumptuous dinner at this, the most expensive and romantic restaurant in Virginia City, Nevada.

Dolly Beavers burped sweetly. "Only three years since we first said hello. It seems as though I've known you all my life, Derby Dear."

"Darby," he corrected patiently. *"Really,* it would mean a lot if you could ever get my first name straight."

"Oh, a name," she sighed. "What does it really matter when two people are as well-matched as we?"

Darby shrugged his massive shoulders, then withdrew one of his Cuban cigars and lit it with relish. "Well," he conceded, "you are right, of course, and I do have somewhat of a reputation as the Derby Man."

It was true. In Wyoming and Nevada, men were beginning to know him by that name and overlook his eastern dress and manners. Why, no cowboy had tried to rope his black derby in over a year.

Dolly reached across the table and squeezed his twenty-two-inch biceps, then shivered with unconcealed admiration. "I'll bet you are the strongest man in the world!"

"No, I don't think I'm quite . . ."

"And you're even a bare knuckles champion!"

"Ex bare knuckles champion," he admitted modestly. "That was a few years ago."

"Phooey. You could win the crown today if you wanted."

1

"Perhaps. But I'm out of training at 255 pounds."

Dolly shrugged as though that were no weight at all for a man almost 5'10" to carry. Besides, it was almost all muscle and Darby needn't fight ever again. "You're too modest, my dear. Everyone knows you're the most famous dime novelist in the world."

He loved to hear Dolly talk like this. And tonight she seemed enchantingly, enticingly beautiful.

"Here's to you!" Dolly proclaimed as she hoisted the dregs of their second bottle of French champagne and motioned to him to join the toast. "To my Darby Buckingham, whose fame is already legendary and who is known to all men!"

Their glasses clinked a bit too exuberantly, splashing some wine, but neither noticed as they gazed at each other with growing passion.

"Dolly?"

"Yes, love?"

"Would you—"

"Excuse me," a tall, handsome man interrupted. "The waiter pointed me in this direction. I'm seeking a . . . ." he read the address on the envelope in his hand, " . . . a Darby Buckingham. Can you point the fellow out? He's supposed to be some kind of a writer, I think."

Darby's black mustache bristled with real irritation. What fame? Legendary to all men? Poppycock! He sure wasn't awing this young lout!

"I'm Darby Buckingham," he snapped. "And I'll ask you to explain the purpose of this rude intrusion."

The man bowed slightly toward Dolly, noting with appreciation the still, very lovely face, the sensual lips and golden hair. His eyes did not miss the voluptuous figure, either. "My apologies," he said to her with a faint smile tugging at the corners of his lips.

"Damn your apologies!" Darby raged, coming to his feet. If this impudent young gallant didn't quit leering at Dolly Beavers, he was going to get his eyes crossed—permanently.

"Sir, my name is Philip Rait the Third and I have a *very* important message."

"I don't care if you're the third or thirtieth Rait," Darby blustered, "your method of introduction requires refinement."

The young man's cheeks colored enough to be seen even in the flickering candlelight. Darby noticed Rait's clenched fists. Good, he thought, perhaps a little after-dinner exercise and a lesson in manners was in order here.

But Philip Rait III regained his composure and, as quick as his temper had flared, it died.

"Again, my apologies."

This time he was addressing Darby and the writer grudgingly accepted.

"But, you see, I have come on an urgent mission to seek your help."

"*My* help? Why me?"

"Actually, I don't need you at all, but the President of the Central Pacific Railroad feels otherwise."

"Mister Charles Crocker?" Darby frowned. "I don't even know the man."

"He knows *you,* Mister Buckingham. Charles Crocker is a great admirer of your work and was most impressed by your chronicling of the Pony Express."

Darby suddenly smiled widely. "How can I be of service?"

"By reading this missive and agreeing to help my employer."

Darby took the letter. He couldn't begin to imagine how he could assist Charles Crocker.

"I'm checked into your hotel," Rait said in a business-like manner. "I'll be waiting—and hoping—that you'll be accompanying me across the Sierras in the morning."

"What!" Dolly cried. "That's out of the question!"

"I see." Rait's expression and tone became filled with resignation. "What a pity. Mister Crocker did so want, and need, your help. I told him you wouldn't be interested, but he wouldn't listen." He reached for the letter. "I guess you won't be needing that, sir."

"Wait a minute," Darby said peevishly. "This is *my* decision, not Miss Beaver's."

"Oh, Darby! I won't stand for another delay."

"Quiet, please Dolly. I have to at least read the blasted thing. I'd go mad with curiosity wondering what could be so important to the President of the Central Pacific Railroad that he needs me desperately."

"Nothing could be. Don't you see! It's all a plot!"

"Plot? What *are* you babbling about, dear woman?"

"It *is* a plot. Someone doesn't want you ever to propose marriage to me."

Tears sprang from her eyes and Darby was afraid she was going to start blubbering. That was always a very unforgettable experience. *No one* could cry like Dolly; her breath seemed to catch in her nose and the wheezing sobs became almost swinelike grunts. Darby patted her on the shoulder.

"Dolly, all I want to do is to *read* the letter. Surely you understand that a man like Mister Crocker deserves at least a response. After all, he did send young Rait the Third clear over the Sierra Nevadas."

"All right," she sniffed.

Rait brightened. "Thank you both." He hailed a passing waiter. "Two more bottles of your best champagne for Mister Buckingham and the lovely lady, courtesy of the Central Pacific Railroad!"

Darby started to protest but then saw the envious faces of all the other patrons and, when he looked back, young Rait had disappeared. Oh, why not, he decided. If they didn't drink them here, they could always smuggle them up to his room, where he and Dolly would continue the party in more intimate surroundings.

Darby opened the letter.

"What does it say?" Dolly asked with real suspicion.

He pressed the letter down on the table, smoothing it neatly and then he began to read.

Dear Mister Darby Buckingham:

I have read of your western exploits with great interest and delight these past years. In particular, I found your involvement with the Pony Express to be singularly remarkable.

The Pony Express was a great accomplishment; yet, I dare say it is nothing compared to the epic contest which our Central Pacific Railroad is about to undertake. No railroad in the world has attempted to assault the equal of the towering Sierra Nevada Mountains. There are substantial numbers of Congressmen who deem the feat impossible. We are most eager to prove them wrong.

However, it is with gravest concern that I write

now, for I desperately need your assistance. We have not yet been underway a year and already we are plagued by unexplained mishaps and accidents. I suspect sabotage.

It is for this reason I now seek your help, Mister Buckingham. If you would consent to join our effort, I feel confident that your reporting would draw the public's eye to our difficulties and perhaps even forestall the efforts of those who might wish us to fail.

In return for your services, I offer you the greatest story being made anywhere in the world. You would have complete access to our documents and very satisfying accommodations in which to pen your story. There is, however, one word of caution I feel bound to relate. If sabotage is being perpetrated and if it were discovered that you were sent to expose the skullduggery, your life may be in forfeit.

Dolly grabbed him by the sleeve. "Oh, Darby, you can't accept his offer! Not if what he says is true."

"Calm yourself, my dear. As you very well know, I'm not one who fears danger." He saw her eyes widen with alarm and added hastily, "But I would only chronicle the event, not become a participant."

"I don't believe you anymore," she whimpered. "You're always getting beat up or worse while 'chronicling' your stories."

Darby scowled. He'd never been whipped—well, at least not in an even fight. "Dolly, compose yourself and allow me to finish Mister Crocker's letter."

As President of the Central Pacific, I would give you my full assistance and protection. I also promise you a race, Mister Buckingham. A race the likes of which has never been seen. Once we cross this formidable mountain range, the Central Pacific will fly eastward across your Nevada deserts to link, at some point, with our rival, the Union Pacific. But, in the meantime, these Sierras await. So be it! We will conquer Donner Pass or die trying, as did the wayfarers on that ill-fated wagon train before us!

Do you dare accept this challenge, Mister Buckingham? I sincerely hope so and am certain the President of the United States, Mister Abraham Lincoln, would also be grateful (a personal copy of this letter is being forwarded to his office).

Please be advised that my confidential secretary, Mister Philip Rait III, is commissioned to bring back either your apology—or your person. I enthusiastically trust it to be the latter. We require your help as I believe you need our great story.

Will you join the contest?

> *Respectfully,*
> *Charles Crocker, President*
> *Central Pacific Railroad*

Darby's hands were trembling when he finished reading. "Did you hear that?" he whispered. "President Abraham Lincoln *needs* me. I *must* answer his command!"

"What command? All it said was that he'd get a copy of Mister Crocker's letter. Oh, Darby, you can't leave now!"

She leaned forward and winked provocatively. "Besides, I thought you and I were going up to your room and continue our party."

He swallowed noisily. The promise—or its denial—was never more clear.

"Couldn't I . . ."

"Have it both ways? Not a chance, Derby, dear. You've been promising me a trip to San Francisco. It's now or never. I've been waiting for three years. Hang Mister Crocker and his railroad! I need you more than the Central Pacific."

"Dolly! Try to understand. The *country* needs me. Our President . . ."

"Has younger men far better trained to do this sort of thing," Dolly interrupted. "Let someone else risk his life for a change."

Darby stood up. "I can't. You know that. Be reasonable, woman."

She shook her head and reached into her purse, yanking

out a hanky. Then she blew her pretty nose lustily. When Dolly peered up at him, her blue eyes were wet and glistening.

"I've ... I've always waited for you. Supported your need to record the history of the west. But ... but well, I don't want to become an old maid."

"Dolly ..."

"No!" she cried. "Just go and let me be for now."

"Will you ... Dolly, I can't ask you to wait again. But will you?" It seemed, to Darby, the most important question he'd ever asked.

"I don't know if I can," she whispered. Then, with tears streaming down her cheeks, she examined the face of the man she loved. "If I said I couldn't, you'd still go. Wouldn't you?"

He *couldn't* lie. "I'd have to. It's why I came west. My readers—it's what they've come to expect."

"I know. And it's what makes me love you," she told him sadly. "So ... so, go on and pack. When you have time, write and tell me everything."

A great flood of gratitude welled up inside of Darby and he kissed her with everyone looking.

"Go on," she breathed, hugging him tight enough to dislodge vertebrae in an ordinary man's neck. "Just promise me one thing."

"Name it."

"When you and that Central Pacific Railroad get over those mountains and reach Nevada, you'll put me on it and carry me off to San Francisco."

"I promise," he vowed. "We're already the same as booked."

"On our honeymoon?"

Darby blinked. Felt the sweat pop from his pores. He loved her, but ...

"Never mind," she said with a brave grin. "I'll settle for one promise at a time."

He reached back and pried her fingers loose behind his neck. "We'd better go. Crocker's man is waiting for an answer."

"Uh-uh," Dolly said. "You go ahead."

"But what about you?"

She poured a full glass of champagne. "I'll be along. But

first . . . first, I think I'll just sit here and wonder how I got talked into waiting through another one of your great adventures."

He smiled. "Cheer up, girl. I'll talk to Philip, then come back immediately."

She nodded, her chin up, but quivering. "You do that. I'll keep the party going."

"Well, Mister Buckingham! Come in. Have you reached your decision?"

Darby waited until Philip Rait closed the door. "On my way over to this hotel, I decided that I would not be able to accompany you back."

Rait looked shocked but recovered quickly. "What a pity. Mister Crocker will be most disappointed. However, he'll respect your decision. Actually, it's probably for the best anyway. Stick to your dime novels. We'll find someone who . . ."

Darby interrupted, "I intend to go—but alone."

"What! Mister Buckingham—why?"

Darby took a chair and lit a Cuban cigar. "If I'm to uncover or discount acts of sabotage, I need to pose as an itinerant laborer seeking work."

"That's ridiculous!" Rait exploded. "Mister Crocker and I agree that your reportage will probably discourage further skullduggery."

"And what if it doesn't?"

Rait studied him for a moment, then shrugged helplessly. "I don't know."

"Of course, you don't. You'd be in dire circumstances. No," the writer said firmly, "we can't take that risk. I intend to hire on as a laborer and work in secret until I'm convinced I've gotten the truth."

"Do you . . ." Rait fumbled for words, and seemed ill at ease.

"Speak up, man. This is no time for artful discretion."

"Very well." The young man's shoulders lifted and his dark, intense eyes bored from his lean, swarthy face. "Do you really think you can withstand the grueling work of grading roadbeds or laying track?"

Darby's thick black eyebrows drew down over his nose until they met. "Mister Rait the Third, I can work any man you've got into the ground. My strength defies the ordinary individual's imagination."

Rait blinked in astonishment. "Ah, yes," he said quietly, "now I remember. You were once a circus strongman. But that was years ago."

Darby didn't care for the implication one bit. "Correct," he said, "I've grown stronger since." Then he got up and headed for the door.

"We shall see, Mister Buckingham. The person you'll ask for a job is Harvey Strobridge. He's a grueling taskmaster. A driver of men. With all respect, he'll work you into the dirt, sir."

Darby yanked the door open and slammed it against the wall. "A thousand dollars says I last until we've beaten Donner Pass."

Rait laughed. "I'll write for money and tell my father I've got a sure bet. Mister Buckingham, you are no longer a young man. I would think you'd know better by now."

Darby grinned maliciously. "Would you care to test your little theory?" he asked, raising his fighter's knuckles.

"Uh-uh. The thousand dollars will be sufficient instruction. Good night. I'll tell Mister Crocker of your . . . plan. He'll keep your stateroom open and waiting, I'm sure."

"Blast!" Darby raged, as he barreled down the hallway. What did that impudent young idiot know about strength and grit? Philip Rait the Third, indeed! Probably a stuffy young easterner whose father's money had gotten him employment. Well, he'd teach young Rait a lesson.

By the time he returned to Dolly, he was still angry. But not Dolly. She was giddy as a girl and twice as lovely. And, as he helped her outside to go for a sobering walk under the blanket of silvery Nevada stars, Darby guessed he shouldn't have allowed himself to become so furious.

Besides, if he was going to pose as a laborer, it meant that he'd be without Crocker's protection. And, if there was a concerted group of scoundrels intent on destroying the Central Pacific, they surely wouldn't have any compulsions about eliminating him in the foulest manner possible. Yes, by his own decision, he'd greatly compounded his personal danger.

"Derby?"

They'd strolled out to the end of C Street to gaze at the thousands of campfires which flickered like fireflies on the slopes of Sun Mountain. The Comstock had attracted fortune hunters from all over the world.

"Yes, dear?"

Dolly rested both hands on his powerful shoulders. "Come back safe to me?"

"Don't I always?"

She smiled a little crookedly and nestled her head against his barrel-chest. "Yes," Dolly whispered. "You always do. And . . . and, well, I feel so much better knowing you'll be living in a stateroom car, protected by Mister Crocker."

Darby glanced up at the moon. It was like a silver ship floating through eternity.

His mind slipped back to the challenge which would begin tomorrow. He'd have none of Crocker's protection. Nor a stateroom. But then, maybe Crocker was wrong about the sabotage. Perhaps the accidents *were* due to Strobridge's incompetence.

Yet, the more he thought about it the more Darby had a gut feeling that the Central Pacific construction boss wasn't to blame for the fledgling railroad's mysterious accidents and that treachery, and even murder, awaited just beyond the mountains.

Chapter 2

The stage ride from Virginia City was uneventful. Darby watched Gold Hill and Silver City pass by as they dropped off the Comstock onto the high desert and into Carson City. A quick change of horses and a bite of food, then he and Philip Rait were hustled back into the stage. They careened through Mormon Station, where the driver reined from south to west, and they attacked the rugged eastern slope of the Sierras. Higher and higher they struggled until, finally, they crested the summit and the driver pulled the lathered team to a halt for a well-earned breather.

Darby and Rait alighted into the crisp mountain air and gazed in wonder at the contrast between the country they'd just left behind and what lay ahead. To the east, Nevada stretched into the barren distance. Except for the green Carson Valley at their feet, the rest of the panorama was a mottled brown and purple vista of stark emptiness. A land Darby well-remembered from his experiences with the Pony Express. This, too, was the country which the Central Pacific would have to beat in order to lay its tracks eastward. If Charles Crocker and Harvey Strobridge thought that the Sierras were their only real obstacle, they hadn't seen the desolation of central Nevada.

Philip Rait stretched his legs and gazed to the west. "Compared to where we've come from, what's ahead is paradise."

It was true. As Darby pivoted to look, the lush contrast of the western slopes was immediately evident. Forty-Niner gold country was as verdant and inviting as the Garden of Eden. He could see rivers dancing toward the valleys below, their waters glistening in the sun. And just to the north lay the jewel of the Sierras, Lake Tahoe. It was stunningly clear, deceptively deep and surrounded by towering forest. Magnificent to behold in any man's eye, Darby could not help but feel a profound awe in the mirror of its beauty.

"All aboard, gents. We're going to make Hangtown by supper."

Darby and Rait clambored aboard and the writer offered his traveling companion a cigar which was declined.

"Tell me, Mister Rait, why didn't Mister Crocker just dispatch a special messenger with that letter, instead of his right-hand man?"

Rait shrugged. "Believe me, I didn't volunteer for the job. But Mister Crocker worried that his letter might be intercepted, placing you into danger."

"Come, now. Aren't you exaggerating this whole situation somewhat?" Darby waited for the man's reaction. If he expected Rait to deny the accusation, he was to be disappointed.

"I think . . . can we assume this conversation is not to be repeated?"

"By all means. Speak freely."

"Good," Rait said. "If you want my opinion, this whole idea of sending for you was a mistake. There is no sabotage. Only the expected amount of bumbling, miscalculations, inefficiencies and confusion."

Darby frowned. "How can you be certain?"

"I can't. And I readily admit that I'm a financial expert, not a railroad builder. Yet, Mister Crocker doesn't seem to realize that one man—Harvey Strobridge—cannot control or oversee two thousand construction laborers."

Darby frowned. "And that's what he's trying to do? Surely he must have foremen."

"Oh, yes. He has them all right. Mostly illiterate Irish. They can't read their own names, much less an engineer's drawings."

"Then they must be replaced!"

"By whom?" Rait asked pointedly. "We can't attract men because they keep running off to the Comstock. My God, Mister Buckingham, the California gold rush is over but gold fever remains. You can't imagine how every rumor of a new strike—anywhere—sends our laborers, and even educated men who ought to know better, running away in the night."

"I see," Darby muttered in a troubled voice. "But what about all the accidents?"

Rait looked at him evenly. "About par for this line of work. We can't retain employees. Everyone is inexperienced. There's bound to be accidents under those conditions."

"But can't some precautions be taken?"

"Like what?" Rait demanded. "The men have to use black powder and that's always risky. People get blown up. Especially when the profit-takers infiltrate our camps and sell their bad whiskey."

"Ban your employees from drinking!" Darby exclaimed. "If they're lighting fuses, they must be steady."

Rait laughed. "Have you ever attempted telling a group of Irishmen they can't spend their wages on drink, women or cards?"

"No."

"Don't try it, Mister Buckingham. They feel pretty strongly that their free time and money are their own. Mister Crocker got so angry he told the whiskey peddlers he'd destroy their stock the next time they brought it to our camps."

"What happened?"

"The crews—Irish, Mexican, all of them—got so mad they went on strike."

"The devil they did!"

"For a fact. And, after a week or so, most of them were Comstock bound. We had to meet their demands or they'd all have left."

Darby thought about it a moment, then glanced up. "So you think it's gold fever and the rule of Harvey Strobridge which is behind the inexperience of your crews. This accounts for the accidents. In short, you don't believe there's any sabotage at all."

"Precisely. That's why I feel it's ridiculous for you to go to all this bother of posing as an ordinary working man."

There was an unmistakable arrogance in Rait's tone that grated badly on Darby's sensibilities. "There's nothing more noble than an 'ordinary' working man doing honest work with his honest hands," Darby gritted.

"Fine, Mister Buckingham. If you choose to join the unwashed masses, that's your business. Perhaps you feel in their debt because they purchase your dime novels, but . . ."

Darby lunged across the coach, grabbed Philip Rait by the lapels and then threw him back into his seat. He shook the man like a terrier would a rat.

"Don't ever talk down to me or the working people again," he warned with cold menace. "Because if you should, I shall throttle you within an inch of your arrogant young life. Do you understand me, Philip?"

"Yes!" Rait croaked. "Let go!"

Darby shoved the man back against the cushions with disgust. "I don't understand what possible reason a man like Charles Crocker has in keeping you on the payroll."

Rait's eyes focused across the dim coach with pure hatred. "My uncle will hear of this, Mister Buckingham. And, I guarantee you, he will not be pleased. In fact, you would be well-advised to disembark at the next stage stop and return to Virginia City!"

"You'd like that, wouldn't you?" Darby chuckled. He felt much better now that he'd scared the wits out of this ill-mannered fool. "Well, I'm afraid you are out of luck, because I'm not about to return unless your uncle orders me to do so. I intend to pocket your wagered money, Philip. One thousand dollars. And I'll get to the truth of things or I'll eat my derby."

"Boiled or breaded?" Rait snickered. "I can hardly wait."

Darby left the stagecoach above Hangtown, although he could have ridden another ten miles. But he was seething at Rait and afraid he might lose his temper and seriously harm the fool. Besides, the strenuous fifty mile hike to the railroad construction site would give him a chance to toughen his legs and become accustomed to exertion at higher altitudes. He needed the exercise. After only a few miles it became clear that he was sadly out of condition. No matter, he thought grimly as he trudged onward, the bet was made and he had no intention of losing.

Yet, as the afternoon wore on into early evening, he was beginning to think he'd been perhaps a bit rash. It seemed as if every vagrant who passed him on the road walked up these hills like a goat with scarcely a puff. True, he was stronger, but his lungs were proving themselves inferior.

Near sunset, Darby realized that he was without food

or bedding and the night air was growing chill. Even in summer, these infernal mountains grew cold and foreboding. Far away, lightning raked the sky and made the ground quiver. Darby swallowed his apprehension, tried to ignore his growling belly and pushed on with great determination toward a trail of smoke which filtered out of the trees some distance away. If he could reach it before darkness, he would prevail upon its owners to feed and bed him in exchange for a generous fee which he'd happily pay.

It seemed forever before he got close enough to hear voices. When he finally did, he noticed they were angry ones. Darby slowed his pace and moved forward with as much stealth as he possessed. And when he knelt down behind a thick pine tree and studied the encampment below, it was twilight and difficult to recognize immediately the cause of the trouble.

He moved in still closer, then his mustache bristled as he realized what was taking place downhill in the neat little Chinese camp beside the flowing river.

"Get over here, you yellow heathen!" a tall, powerful man with a thick beard ordered, as he sliced the air with a foot-long Bowie knife. "I'm goin' to slice off your goddamn pigtail just like the rest—unless you'd rather I open your gullet."

The young Chinaman facing him shook his head solemnly. Like his band of companions, he was small in stature and couldn't have weighed more than one hundred pounds. He wore a pajama-like shirt and trousers of pale blue and a basket-shaped woven hat. He looked scared but determined. "You cut hair, very bad for China boy."

"Yeah, so I heard. Means your spirit wanders through hell a'howling—or something like that, if you die. Well, you will die if you don't get over here, egg sucker."

The Chinaman gazed at the pile of hacked queues lying in the dirt and the lowered heads of his countrymen who'd already been forced to submit to this outrage.

"No, please. No cut."

The man with the knife shrugged, then winked at one of his companions. "Shoot him, Willard. We can say he and these others all jumped our claim."

"It our claim!"

"The hell you say! This here is American soil and you little thieves are working the South Fork of the *American*

River. You're Chinamen! What gives you the right to come over here and take our gold?"

"You no work anymore. White men all gone. Gold all gone, except for little."

"Yeah, well, if it's so damn little, why do you people keep moving up into this country and reworking the old placer claims?"

"Chen Yun speak for all when he say we a small people. Eat little. Work hard. Only take little gold you no want."

"The hell you say!" He swiveled to his partners. "Say, Willard. Buck. Either of you boys ever see any gold you 'no want'?"

The two other men laughed outright, while Darby began to edge forward.

"Tell you what, Chen Yun. Since you seem to be the mouthpiece for this scurvey group of yellow scum, I'll give you a choice. Hand over all your gold and you can keep your hair piece. Same goes for the rest of 'em we haven't touched."

Chen Yun faced his people and began talking to them in Chinese. To Darby, it seemed as if he was asking them to do something more than hand over their gold. Yet, he couldn't be sure. The six or seven who'd already submitted said nothing; it was as if their manhood had been taken instead of just their hair. But the rest argued violently.

"Well, what's it to be! Gold or pigtails?" the knife-wielder stormed.

Chen Yun's back straightened. He revolved as the clattering voices grew silent.

"I tell them what you say. They do not believe."

"Oh yeah!" Willard exclaimed, cocking his pistol. "Well maybe they'll believe when I put a hole through your skinny chest!"

Darby Buckingham had no particular feelings either way for the Chinaman, yet he couldn't ignore this injustice. What was about to happen was thievery and cold-blooded murder. He reached into his valise and fumbled around until he located his derringer. It was a .41 caliber Remington and its single bullet was plenty big enough at close range which, for Darby, was essential, given his notoriously poor marksmanship. But, here, he faced three men—not one—and, in the poor light and open encampment, a stray shot would probably hit one of the innocent Celestials.

"Good evening," he hailed as he emerged jauntily from the forest.

Three guns swiveled to line on his chest. Darby smiled his widest and prayed he looked like an innocent passerby.

"Who the hell are you, sneakin' around out there?" the knife-man asked.

"An American, unlike those yellow scum," Darby said, casting a malicious eye in Chen Yun's direction, thus clearly indicating his loyalties. "I see you were about to have some sport. Mind if I join in?"

"Sure as hell do. This is a private party."

Darby kept moving forward, but by all appearances he was intent on the Chinese. He strode up to Chen Yun and jabbed a forefinger into the man's bony chest. "Where'd you learn to speak English, you heathen?"

A veiled look of inscrutability fell over Chen's eyes. "My father was a trader with the English seamen. He taught me."

Darby's lips formed a contemptuous sneer. Then he noticed the faint outline of a heavy chain and medallion which rested under the Chinaman's pale blue shirt.

"What are you wearing?"

"Nothing you would understand."

"Liar!" Darby grabbed the man by the shirtfront, bunching cloth up in his fist. Then he yanked the medallion out for everyone to see.

"Solid gold," he commented drily, turning to look at the three behind him. "You lied to me. Hand it over."

Chen Yun wasn't going to do it. Darby saw the way his eyes sparkled and, before the young man could deliver a blow, the writer released him.

"Hey!" the short, barrel-chested man named Buck yelled as he leapt forward. "Grab him before he runs off!"

Darby grabbed Buck by the arm as he swept by and swung him in a quick half circle. With all his strength, Darby lifted Buck off the ground and hurled him spinning into the other pair.

There was a startled cry as Buck slammed into them and all three went flying. Willard came up first with a gun in his hand and Darby kicked his wrist as the pistol exploded up at the treetops. Willard yelped in pain but Darby cut him off short with a vicious punch between the eyes that knocked him rolling.

The knifeman and Buck came at him as though they'd practiced all their lives. Darby took a punch, grappled with Buck, then used him as a shield as the Bowie knife sliced the air.

"Goddammit, Silas! Don't cut me!"

Silas swore as Darby backed away, wondering what would happen next. When he saw Willard start to get up, he knew he couldn't afford to let both men regroup, then trap him. He did the only thing he could do, and that was to charge Silas using Buck as a shield.

The move came as a surprise and Silas tried to thrust the Bowie knife around his friend into Darby's ribs. It didn't work. The writer felt his coat rip away, then he clamped an elbow down on Silas' wrist and pivoted, throwing all his weight sideways. They landed hard and Buck screamed as they rolled.

"I'm cut! You cut me!"

Silas gaped at the smaller man and at the flesh wound across his rounded shoulders as Darby punched him flatfooted, right in the mouth. Yellow teeth caved in against his knuckles and, as Silas dropped the knife and grabbed at his ruined face, Darby whistled an uppercut to his midsection that lifted the tall man a foot off the ground.

Willard was back in operation and he came in fast with a boot that struck Darby on the kneecap and knocked him down hard. Before he could recover, another kick buried itself in his stomach and caused the air to gush out of his lungs.

Willard grabbed the fallen knife and turned it edge up. "Now," he panted, "I'm going to finish what Silas couldn't. Grab him round the neck, Buck, and pull his head back so his neck is ready."

Buck, driven by hatred and realizing his own wound wasn't nearly as serious as he'd first thought, moved in with relish for his task.

Darby reached inside for his derringer and realized with horror that it was gone! In fact, the entire coat pocket was torn away.

While Silas choked and spat teeth, Buck and Willard advanced on the gasping writer. He wasn't going to outrun them and, right now, that Bowie knife seemed at least a yard long. Darby struggled to his feet, then backed up against a pine tree. It looked as though he was at the end of the line.

"Come on," he rasped.

As he steeled himself for the knife blade, Darby heard a whirring noise not unlike that of a rope being twirled fast through the air; then, the sound of the Chinese war axe as it buried itself between Willard's shoulder blades. The man's eyes distended, he took a faltering step, then another, as his expression registered astonishment. The Bowie knife slipped from his spasming fingers; one hand tried to reach back and grab at the thing that drove him down.

Buck yelled as his partner swiveled and then crashed to the pine needles, dead before his face struck the earth.

The two who remained fled in terror, leaving big Willard. And Darby Buckingham's eyes met those of Chen Yun.

"You will stay, please?"

The question caught Darby by surprise. He leaned back against the pine tree and allowed the tension to drain from his battered body.

"Yes," he said quietly. "I am hungry and tired. I would like to rest here."

"Good!" The Chinaman actually smiled. "You fool Chen Yun and the bad men."

"Yeah," Darby said, easing away from the tree. "But I almost didn't pull it off this time."

He strode over to where his coat had been ripped and, when he bent over to retrieve the derringer, a sharp pain rifled through his knee.

Chen Yun was instantly at his side, giving orders to the others. Moments later, Darby was stretched out on a soft pile of clean blankets, watching a pair of Chinese apply steaming poultices to his swollen knee.

"This will feel better. Much better," Chen Yun said, handing him a cup of tea that had a delicious molasses taste he savored. "Can you eat now?"

Darby grinned. "Can an Irishman drink whiskey?"

Chen Yun must have understood, because he giggled and issued several orders. Darby watched the Chinese scurry around the campfire. The things he smelled were promising. And, even if the food were strange, it wouldn't matter. He was hungry enough to eat the lice off a hibernating bear.

Chapter 3

Darby remained in the Chinese camp for two days. He relaxed and waited until the swelling in his knee was gone. The rest was welcome and he found the Chinese to be a cleanly people and the most industrious workers he'd ever come across.

They were also quite ingenious when it came to reclaiming the played-out rivers for gold. Their method was to throw wet sand onto the bank until it dried, then spread it on tightly woven circular blankets around which they gathered. At a signal, they would began rippling and blowing the dried sand between them, until they'd managed to bounce all the sand and gravel away, leaving only the heavier gold. Once, Darby tried his hand at the process and found it extremely difficult to keep from tossing everything to the ground. But the Chinese seemed to consider it a game, although, at the end of the day, the labor of the fifty or so men amounted to no more than an ounce or two of gold—not nearly enough to entice an American to have a try at these claims.

Even so, Chen Yun explained that they were constantly being harassed by outsiders. "They seem to wish us dead, Mister Buckingham. Even though we work only the leavings, there is always much trouble for our people."

Darby nodded, "I can't see how all of you can begin to feed yourselves."

"Much gold has been found where there was thought to be none. We survive, although each year it becomes more difficult. There are many Chinamen who come to these rivers."

"What happens when even you people can't reclaim enough gold to survive?"

Chen Yun shrugged almost fatalistically. "Perhaps we go back to our homeland. But there, too, hunger stalks with long teeth."

Speaking of hunger, Darby was in good form. Perhaps it was the mountain air which whetted his appetite. Whatever, in a very short time he'd become proficient with a pair of chopsticks and, while he would have enjoyed a steak and potatoes, along with some good ale to wash it down, the Chinese diet of rice, mushrooms, salted cabbage, vermicelli and bamboo sprouts was cooked to perfection and served to him in big steaming pots.

When the time came for him to leave, Chen Yun reached under his shirt and lifted the gold chain and heavy round medallion. It almost covered the palm of Chen's hand and Darby saw that it was beautifully carved in relief, with a picture of the sun shining over a peaked mountain beside which a lion rested.

"I can't take this," Darby whispered.

"You must," Chen Yun told him. "It is a tradition in my family to give the thing you most prize when your life has been saved by another."

"Yes, but . . ." Darby tried to find words that would make this young man realize that he couldn't accept the medallion in good conscience.

Chen Yun continued. "The engraved legend tells of a young man who journeyed up the mountain in search of God." He turned it over so that Darby could see the back side.

"What does that mean?" Darby saw a slain deer around which a long snake had wrapped itself.

"It means the boy may find the courage of the lion and reach great heights with God as is shown on the other side of this, or he may fall among serpents if his heart is weak and he fails to reward those who would protect his life."

"I see. But those three men . . ."

"Were serpents," Chen Yun interrupted quietly. "You saved my life and must take this. For me to wear it now would be a curse."

"Thank you," Darby said, his voice thickening with emotion. It was the most beautiful gift he'd ever received, and the realization that there was more gold in the chain and medallion than these poor men would probably extract in weeks, moved the writer deeply.

He placed it around his neck. "I will wear it proudly, Chen Yun."

The young man smiled, bowed with respect and said, "Go then, Darby Buckingham. If you ever need our humble assistance, you have only to show the medallion to my people."

"I'll remember," he promised. Darby pivoted to leave, his bag in hand. "One thing I have to know."

"Ask."

"Why did you come to this distant country? You're an educated man with a family of great standing. Why leave for . . . this?"

Chen Yun blinked. "China very old and America very young. People starve, even in the great rice regions of Kwangtung Province on the Canton Delta. I speak English and come with these people to help them live. I teach them your language. They are all young men who learn fast."

"And you. Will you return to China?"

"In spirit," Chen Yun said, "I have never gone."

Darby nodded. He slipped the gold medallion under his collar and waved farewell. All fifty of them bowed and said "Goodbly, Darbly Bucklingham!"

He grinned, then left them for he, as they, had a job waiting.

Early that day, he passed through the valley settlement of Coloma and noted with interest the remains of Sutter's Mill, where James Marshall had discovered gold more than a decade ago and had set off the greatest stampede of fortune-seekers in the history of western civilization. The sawmill was abandoned now, as well as dozens of rickety buildings and shacks where thousands once had swarmed. If memory served, the fabulous discovery had been a curse to Sutter, because hordes had overrun his prosperous lands, slaughtered his cattle and left him financially ruined. It was said James Marshall had fared as badly.

Darby stopped at a small, failing dry goods store where an old arthritic proprietor sold him food, bedding and work clothes. He'd need them if he didn't reach the construction site by dark and, even if he did, his eastern suit, pressed collar and round-toed shoes would have been hard to explain.

As he was paying, Darby ventured a question. "Whatever happened to James Marshall?"

"I couldn't say."

"Well, do you know someone who might know his story? I'm a writer and . . ."

"Then write his obituary," the store owner graveled. " 'Cause if he ain't dead yet, he will be soon. James Marshall climbed into a whiskey bottle years ago. He'll never come out alive. That's all I know."

"I see." Darby shook his head.

"What are you going to do with that suit, shoes and the derby hat, mister?"

"I hadn't thought about it." One thing sure, he wouldn't be taking them to the railroad camps.

"Give you a bottle of whiskey for 'em."

"I'd rather hear about Marshall and Sutter."

"Told ya I don't know about either of 'em."

Darby looked away. Damned if there wasn't a story here and if his curiosity wasn't running free about the two ill-fated discoverers. Maybe he'd come back and pick up the threads of those two men's lives and see where they had unraveled.

"You want to swap or don't you?"

"Sure," he said, "but make it your very best, because I mean to share it with none other than the President of the Central Pacific Railroad."

The storekeeper frowned, but the whiskey he handed over had a label and that meant it wasn't home brew, which would have been asking too much of Charles Crocker.

As it turned out, Darby needn't have worried about the quality of the whiskey. It was mid-afternoon when he reached the North Fork of the American River and he was bent over the churning torrent when the first bullet screamed flat across the white water's surface and slammed into his chest, knocking him sideways. The bottle of whiskey shattered against the rocks. When Darby pitched into the roaring river, the impact of the bullet, coupled with the icy water, almost proved shockingly fatal. He went under, gasping for air, feeling as though his chest was on fire and knowing he was being twisted into the deeper currents.

He plowed into a submerged tree and felt its great soggy roots clutch at his body, trying to strangle away what life remained. Darby clawed and ripped at the branches until they released him to churn downriver. With his last driving will to survive, the writer managed to break to the surface. His mouth flew open to haul in great draughts of air as he splashed and bounced up against a rock, struggling to gain the shore. The current pinned him like a bug on a specimen board.

Searching bullets pinged off the rocks, then ricocheted into the forest. Darby glanced upriver and saw a man hopping from boulder to boulder, trying to gain a clear target. He was tall and lean and carrying a rifle. But, as Darby tried to channel his vision clear, his weight shifted and the current snatched him away and carried him spinning downriver.

The echo of gunfire was far behind when Darby finally reached a wider spot in the river and paddled wearily to safety. He lay in the mud watching a cloud of gnats buzz around his face for almost ten minutes before he rolled over and clambored to his feet.

Everything he owned was gone, lost in the treacherous water. Except for the wad of soggy bills in his pocket, the only thing he possessed of value was the medallion. He checked it to be certain and, when he did, he noticed the bullet's crater-like depression.

"Well, I'll be damned!" he whispered, understanding now why that first slug hadn't killed him outright. Darby pushed the medallion back under his wet shirt and trudged toward higher ground. He figured the rifleman was none other than Silas and he guessed he should have anticipated some kind of reprisal.

Even now, as he left the river and hiked up toward a vantage point, he wondered about the other, short man, the one named Buck. He'd been cut, yet not badly. Perhaps Buck was waiting somewhere up ahead. Darby swallowed drily. Hellfire, he didn't even have his trusty derringer anymore. Except for his muscle and wits, he was as helpless as a babe in the woods.

Later that evening, footsore and tired, he topped a hill and saw the Central Pacific Railroad under construction. It was an impressive sight and a far bigger project than he'd expected. Darby estimated that more than a thousand men were hard at work, even at this late hour, racing the setting sun, laying track up to a point where a thick granite formation like a buffalo's hump had stopped them cold. But not for long. Even as Darby watched, an army of construction laborers were pounding out a deep gash in the rock.

The sound of black powder explosions punctuated the air and Darby noted how the laborers would rush in to clear away the blasted rock by loading it onto one-horse dump carts and wheelbarrows. No sooner had they scrambled back across an invisible perimeter, when another explosion would shower more rock into the sky.

From his vantage point, Darby noticed other workers further east of the granite hump, busily laying track and grading the roadbed with shovel and pick. Beyond them, a distance of some two or three miles, he could see men crawling like ants on a trestle which spanned a deep ravine. "So," he whispered, sitting to rest his aching feet, "that's how one builds a railroad. When they hit an obstacle, some take it on, while others bypass and keep the line moving."

Almost at dusk, the big locomotive whistle blew three times and everything came to a halt. Even from a distance, Darby noted a heavy weariness in the laborers as they dropped their tools and trudged toward the tent camps.

Darby stood up and felt the soreness in his protesting muscles. The fight plus the unaccustomed hiking caused him to feel stiff-limbed and battered. Cheer up, he thought as he started down toward the swirl of activity, it won't get any better.

It wasn't hard to locate the traveling car of Charles Crocker. Making sure no one noticed his movement, Darby crossed the tracks and stepped up to knock.

"What the hell is wrong now!" a voice roared.

Darby's black eyebrows raised questioningly. He knocked again. Heavy footsteps pounded inside and the door flew open. The man who stood towering above was big—at least Darby's own weight, but most of it gone to fat. He had thin lips which slanted down at the corners and a flowing goatee which sprouted out of a prominent chin. Crocker looked tough and out of sorts. Darby could smell whiskey on his breath.

"Who the hell are you and what the devil do you want at this hour?"

"Hospitality," Darby replied shortly. "Food. Some of your good whiskey and a job."

"What!" Crocker bellowed. "Why you . . ."

"Let me handle this," came a voice as Philip Rait pushed into the doorway. Then the younger man froze, blinked in astonishment and whispered, "Buckingham. You made it!"

"Of course. Am I to stand out here all night?"

Crocker's eyes widened. *"You're* Darby Buckingham?"

"Didn't Philip tell you I was coming?" The writer scowled at the younger man.

"Why . . . why no, not exactly. He said you started and then disembarked. We both thought you'd changed your mind."

"Obviously, I have not. May I come inside or do you want this entire camp to know the purpose of my arrival?"

"Hell, no! Come on in!" Crocker boomed.

Inside, Darby accepted a drink and the President of the Central Pacific's apologies. He noted with some pleasure that Charles Crocker was mad as hell at his personal secretary for misleading him. Without much ceremony, Philip Rait III was ordered to his own compartment up front. He left the room in an obvious snit, causing Darby no little amusement.

Crocker noticed Darby's smile. "I had a feeling you and he didn't exactly hit it off in Virginia City. But don't mind Philip. He's a good enough boy and he tries hard. He just needs some aging, that's all."

Or a good, manly trouncing, Darby thought.

Crocker splashed whiskey into his own glass. "Damn, I'm glad to see you, Mister Buckingham! Can't tell you how disappointed I was when Philip told me you'd left the stage and probably headed back to Nevada."

"I did it for a reason. Am I wrong in understanding that Philip failed to tell you my intention of working on your construction crew?"

"What! Are you crazy?"

Darby curbed his tongue. "No," he said, "I firmly believe the only way I can possibly determine if there is sabotage or not is to become anonymous."

"But how? You're famous."

"By name. Few have seen my face."

"It's no good," Crocker argued. "My construction superintendent, Harvey Strobridge, is too hard a man for someone like you to work under. In fact, he and I just finished quarreling."

"What about?"

"The way he handles the crews. He treats them like animals. Swears and curses and drives them without pity or letup. Know what he told me?"

Darby shook his head with exasperation. While he didn't want to be specially treated, he sure wasn't going to be degraded by some pompous slavedriver.

"He said he was forced to humiliate and browbeat his workers. He said you couldn't talk to them like gentlemen because they weren't anything of the sort. In fact, he told me most of the crew are nearer to beasts than humans."

"Then," Darby said in a low voice, "I will have to educate your Mister Strobridge."

Crocker smiled. "Don't tangle with him. You'd both get hurt and I need all the help I can get. We've got our hands full trying to slice through Bloomer Cut."

"I saw it. Quite a job."

"It'll get worse," Crocker quipped without humor. "But, even so, we'll make it. Got to. Way back in Nebraska, our rivals, the Union Pacific, are finally getting under way. We get the same Congressional incentives as they do—ten miles of land in alternate sections on either side of the right of way for each mile of connected track, plus loans of $16,000 a mile on the open plains, $32,000 through the Great Basin, and $48,000 a mile over the mountains."

"Sounds generous enough."

"It's not," Crocker said pointedly. "Ted Judah, God rest his driven soul, laid out the finest survey and route that could bridge these mountains. His work was excellent but he badly underestimated our costs, so that when President Lincoln authorized the money under the Pacific Railroad Act, his requests fell short."

"How short?"

"I don't know yet," Crocker said, deep worry lines etched on his corpulent face. "This Bloomer Cut is our first real obstacle since leaving Sacramento. We've spent two months blasting and still haven't gotten deep enough to maintain grade for our engines."

"How much further down?"

"We're almost there now. Our engineers estimate it'll be over sixty feet deep and eight hundred feet long. Try and imagine how expensive that kind of work is per mile. Why, we're spending over ten thousand dollars a day!"

"I see." Darby wanted to redirect the conversation. "Tell me, what real evidence do you have of sabotage?"

Crocker's eyes sparked with fury. "Busted tow chains that send men and animals hurtling over embankments. Black powder that doesn't behave like it should. Fuses soaked in oil so they burn too quickly and blow a man up. Labor agitators trying to stir up a strike. Altered diagrams and drawings so the workmen misconstruct a trestle or grade a false roadbed. You get the idea?"

"Yes. But I'm confused."

"How?"

"Well, Philip Rait said he thought it was a matter of inefficiencies that would be worked out if you could retain an experienced crew."

"Bull!" Crocker spat. "Young Philip is good with money, but he doesn't know a damn thing about construction."

"Then it's untrue?"

Crocker backed down a little. "Not entirely," he reluctantly conceded. "We have a devilish time holding onto a labor crew. Gold fever. Everyone is going to strike paydirt on the Comstock."

"So I've heard."

"But a big part of it is that I'm losing good men because of stupid accidents. Like yesterday morning at six o'clock when—"

"Six o'clock!" Darby gasped. "You actually start work at that barbaric hour?"

"Why, of course. Breakfast line shuts down at five-thirty. That's when we hire the new men and form the work crews."

Darby swallowed. He hadn't thought about getting prodded out of bed at such a dismal hour. "I'd better get to sleep," he said weakly. "It's been a very long day."

Crocker eyed him closely. "Mister Buckingham, if you insist on posing as a laborer, then you have no real idea of how long a day can be."

Darby thought to tell Crocker about how he'd already hiked thirty miles and escaped a near drowning in the treacherous American River. But he didn't. It would only create another worry for the railroad builder and, just maybe, Silas and Buck wouldn't be foolish enough to enter these camps.

"I'll make it," Darby said stubbornly.

"Are you certain I can't tell Harvey? He could give you something easy . . ."

"And every man on his crew would hate the newcomer for stealing a soft job. No thanks. I want to be able to sleep at night without worrying about getting my head bashed."

Crocker nodded gravely. "If anyone realizes you're spying for me, it might happen anyway."

Darby turned to go. "Maybe I'll get lucky and catch the

men you want before they become suspicious. But, if I don't . . . if something should go wrong, contact Dolly Beavers in Virginia City. Tell her my lawyer has my will and I've left everything to her."

"I'll do it, Mister Buckingham, but . . ."

"Good night, sir. I'll talk to you when I have news." He'd cut him off short because Darby was afraid he might be talked into backing out of this mad plan to expose the saboteurs. For right now, as tired and battered as he felt, the whole idea seemed crazy enough to get him murdered.

But he'd made his bet and now he'd play the hand he was dealt. It was just too damned late to back down; besides, President Abraham Lincoln was counting on his best effort— and he'd give it or die trying.

Chapter 4

The locomotive whistle ripped the grey morning stillness with a shriek that almost gave Darby a heart attack. He leapt up in his blankets, twisting around for an assailant and, then, losing his balance, he toppled over in a heap.

"All right. All right! Everyone up and heading for the slop chutes. Come on, just like a bunch of swine!"

Darby growled a rumbling warning and saw the tall, swaggering form of Harvey Strobridge emerge from the chilly gloom.

"Hey, you!"

"What?" Darby asked.

"If you're hunting for work, then look somewhere else," Strobridge ordered.

"Why?" Darby demanded. "I heard you needed men."

"Not your size. I need *young* men. Not fat, middle-aged merchants or whatever the hell you were."

Darby rose to his feet. Strobridge was at least his own age, although his tall, rangy body carried not an ounce of fat over corded muscle.

"I'm strong and used to hard work," he insisted.

"The hell you are!" Strobridge laughed cuttingly. "Stick your paws out."

Darby complied.

"Ha! Just as I thought. You're a goddamn desk polisher if I've ever seen one!"

"Yes, but . . ."

"If you're hungry, you're welcome to eat, but then move on. Idlers are bad for the crew." Strobridge rushed off. "Come on, get up and move or I'll have the cook toss it in the dirt and you can eat like the pigs you are!"

Darby stifled his outrage. What a detestible man! *He* was

the animal. No wonder Strobridge's crew deserted him. Darby decided to chase down the superintendent and set him straight on a few points of decency, but his blankets tangled his feet and he crashed to the earth once more.

"Blast!"

A man nearby rubbed sleep from his eyes. "Meanest boss I ever worked for. You're better off getting turned down. This job ain't fit for a dog."

"I can see that. How's the food?"

"He called it right," the man yawned. "Slop. Fit for pigs. But you can have all you'll eat."

Darby smelled the aroma. Not too bad. Maybe he would have to tuck in his tail and crawl back to Crocker, but first he'd ponder the dilemma on a full belly; Buckinghams always thought better when they weren't hungry.

The long table where they ate had all the tin plates nailed down tightly. The cooks passed along, ladling the slop and slamming down half-baked biscuits that sank to the pit of Darby's stomach like frozen lard-balls. Some of the mostly Irish crew examined him intently because of his enormous bulk. Yet most were still half-asleep and too weary from their labor of past days to take notice. From the few who talked, Darby gathered that the morale of the crew was at rock bottom; the food, though plentiful, was tasteless and never varied, the wages weren't nearly high enough considering the rash of fatal and maiming accidents and, most important of all, they hated the Superintendent of Construction, Harvey Strobridge. The unpleasantness of the meal was heightened by the disagreeableness of those partaking of it. "Strike" was the word most frequently uttered over the cold, congealing gravy they called slop. And, as he looked up and down the long, long table at the hard, fatigue-lined faces, Darby knew they weren't bluffing.

Once again, the locomotive whistle blasted through the sharp morning air and everyone dropped their spoons and headed for work. It was exactly six o'clock. Except for a short lunch break, Strobridge would have them driving into the granite mass called Bloomer Cut for another twelve hours.

A bucket of hot, soapy water sloshed across his plate and drenched Darby's shirt and pants. "What the devil are you doing!" he roared, slamming down his cup of coffee.

"Cleaning the table," a scrawny, bearded fellow snapped.

"Get outa my way or I'll wash you into the gully along with the rest of the garbage."

Darby stood up, grabbed the scullery worker and a second bucket of soap and water. He shoved the man's face down into it—hard. *No one* messed with the Derby Man during his meals. No one! When the fellow began to flop around, Darby let him go and poured himself another cup of coffee before going to retrieve his belongings. It was only a few minutes after six in the morning and already the day seemed old and shot to hell. No wonder. At such a barbaric hour, men were not prone to be mannerly. He needed to smoke and think. Maybe he'd talk to Crocker or even pay that arrogant young Rait the one thousand dollars and be off. Donner Pass was less than eighty miles to the east but, right now, it seemed like eight thousand.

Darby neither visited Crocker nor returned to Virginia City. Instead, he decided to camp up in the hills and watch the railroad's progress for a couple of days. By doing this, he would give himself enough time to figure out how to change Strobridge's mind concerning employment, while also allowing study of the workings of the entire operation. He intended to remain out of sight, trusting that he'd witness some nefarious act and thus uncover sabotage if it was indeed being perpetrated.

Late that afternoon, he hailed a freighter with a string of heavily laden pack mules bound for Washoe and was delighted to be able to purchase two salted hams, potatoes, coffee, cooking utensils, a box of cigars and even a few bottles of whiskey. It cost him more than a hundred dollars but he was grateful to provision himself so lavishly. It would make the period of surveillance so much more pleasant.

That first evening he sat up late, watching the railroad workers' campfires and thinking about what would happen in the days to come. Ideally, he'd see the villains at work and be able to notify Crocker of their identities. That would be easiest for everyone and would allow him to accept the railroad president's luxurious accommodations with a satisfied mind. But what if, after a week or two, he saw accidents that clearly indicated there was no plot? No sabotage? Just incompetence. Would Charles Crocker believe him? Probably not. Yet, there was the possibility that Strobridge would have to be discharged.

So be it, Darby thought. The construction superintendent might be extraordinarily competent at building a railroad, but he certainly didn't know how to handle men. Darby recalled Crocker relating how Harvey Strobridge viewed the laborers as sub-humans, animals to be threatened and driven to the limit of their endurance. Poppycock! Do that and they'd leave him stranded and helpless at the first sign of difficulty.

Late that night, when Darby crawled into his blankets beside the campfire, he decided he'd be forced to teach the superintendent a lesson in management. Building morale and loyalty was the way to get production and, at the same time, preserve human dignity.

Darby gazed, heavily lidded, at the blanket of stars above. If he ever figured a means to get past Strobridge and get hired, he'd use himself as an example to show Strobridge the error of his ways. But first, he had to determine if there really were any saboteurs.

Darby wasn't sure exactly what awakened him late that night. Perhaps it was the scream of a prairie dog as a coyote's fangs pierced its heart. Or maybe the passing night owl's silent wings as they beat the air over his face—or, possibly, that the killer who stalked into his camp simply erred as a twig or rock protested under the sole of his boot. But, for whatever reason, Darby woke, knowing something deadly was close and ready to spring.

For long moments, he lay very still. The smoldering campfire made an occasional popping sound, a bird or bat fluttered across the moon and a boot crunched softly down on the earth. Darby's heartbeat accelerated. His thick, stubby fingers began to inch away from his body toward the campfire ring. Perhaps if he could grab a rock, then . . .

It was too late. In the moonlight, he saw the body silhouetted and the glint of the knife blade.

"Silas!"

Darby twisted as the attacker sailed in a low dive with the knife out in front and pointed toward the throat. The blade flashed and the writer felt its cutting edge burn across his left shoulder.

Then Darby went wild with pain and rabid fury. He rolled again and grabbed a rock, just as the man lunged once more. The knife struck the rock and glanced aside as Darby smashed it into his assailant's face, then engulfed him in his arms and began to crush him. Yet, before he really brought his tremendous strength to bear, the man choked, stiffened, then went slack in Darby's powerful arms.

A ruse?

Darby jerked him hard, but there was no cry of pain—only limpness and a faint catch of the lungs. Then he pushed away and scrambled to throw wood on his campfire so that he might see why his attacker had collapsed so easily.

Moments later, as the flames bit into wood and fired the blackness. Darby rocked back in disbelief. It wasn't Silas at all! A stranger. One with his own knife buried in his chest.

Tearing away the bloody shirt, Darby examined the knife and knew that not even a surgeon could save this man.

"Who are you?" Darby shouted, leaning toward the man's ear. "Why did you try to kill me! For money?"

The lips moved and silently formed a word.

"Louder! Tell me. Quickly!"

Darby pressed close, so close he could feel the lips move, hear the death rattle of the flooding lungs.

"Louder!"

A moment passed. The failing body quivered. The lips fluttered.

"Hate? Did you say hate? Why, why do you hate me!"

The man's head rolled sideways, then he seemed to try to roll it back. Whatever he tried to do, he never succeeded. With a soft sighing noise, he died, the mystery of his action carried away forever.

The next morning when the locomotive blast went off, Darby finished another cup of coffee and rose wearily to his feet. There was now enough daylight to see and he moved away from his camp, searching for the dead man's horse and outfit. While the dew was still heavy enough to bend the grass, he searched in ever-widening circles but found nothing to indicate where his attacker had come from.

Nothing to the west, south or east. And he couldn't have come up the hill from the . . . Darby froze. *Or could he?*

He backtracked to his campfire and stared at the body as though he might be able to fathom the mystery just by study He'd already checked the pockets for identification and be longings that might give him a clue but had found nothing except a few dollars in change.

Darby looked at the man's palms. Heavily calloused

Anything else? Something that might reveal his background or business in life? Nothing. Nothing except the curious manner in which the upper legs of his trousers were almost worn through. To him this was inexplicable and perhaps meaningless. The important thing now was that it seemed quite possible that this man had come from the Central Pacific camps and tried to murder him in his sleep.

But why?

Again and again, the answer came—the only one that made any sense at all—yet he kept avoiding it until he had no alternative but to admit that his presence was viewed as a threat by someone down in the camp. That could mean only that Charles Crocker was absolutely right; there were saboteurs—and they already knew his purpose!

Darby sat down and lit a cigar. If he held with his original idea of posing as a common worker, he would be a lamb among the pack of wolves. Yet, to give in now and take the easy way out by joining Crocker would eliminate any chance he had at either exposing the villains or getting to know personally those who were building this mighty railroad. And they were the *real* story. Plenty of journalists would fill thousands of pages on Collis Huntington, Leland Stanford, Mark Hopkins, Thomas Durant and the other wealthy railroad barons. No one other than Darby Buckingham—if he stayed and worked knowing his life was in a delicate balance—could possibly chronicle this page of history.

He *had* to stay. Darby would bury this man and leave no trace of passing. The others who waited below would be unsure if their ambassador of death had fled his mission—or failed. If killed, had Darby Buckingham first tortured him into revealing his treacherous fellow saboteurs? Let them wonder! It was the only uncertainty they now faced.

Darby spent most of the rest of the day in patient observation of Harvey Strobridge and his blasting crew. Hazardous work. Drilling holes in the granite, setting the charges of black powder, then lighting the fuses and racing away before the deafening roar.

It was near quitting time and Darby gathered up his belongings and prepared to break camp. He'd decided to have another talk with Mister Strobridge. Perhaps the man would be a bit more civil at the end of the day than at the beginning. Darby hoped so because, all day long, he'd watched the crews labor and he thought he could more than hold his own among them. Sure, there'd be some soreness in his legs—but not in his arms, back or shoulders. In fact, as he noted how it took five men to heft a quarter-ton rail, he found himself wondering if he could move it alone. Maybe. It would be twice his own weight but easy enough to grip and hold. Maybe. Darby kind of wanted to find out.

The sun was dipping into the western horizon when Strobridge ordered the last set of black powder charges placed in Bloomer Cut, then told everyone to knock off for supper. Darby was one of the few watching alongside the man when the charges exploded. Or at least five of the six did.

"Hellfire!" Strobridge roared when the din and dust settled. "Someone go check that fuse."

Darby smiled down from the top of the huge trench. "All your pigs have headed for the slop chutes, Strobridge. It's just you and me and I'm just watching since I have no job."

Strobridge's face went crimson. "You still sneakin' around here and eating off the Central Pacific's hospitality?"

Before Darby could phrase a suitable answer, the construction superintendent was tromping into the cut, hunting for matches to relight the fuse.

Suddenly it flared, when Strobridge was no more than twenty feet away from it.

"Look out!" Darby yelled.

It was too late. Before the railroad superintendent could pivot and run or even shield his face, the rock exploded upward, spewing granite fragments into the air like grape shot from a cannon.

Harvey Strobridge screamed and was hurled thirty feet backward to slam into the rock cut and sag into a crumpled heap of blood and tattered clothing.

Darby raced down into the cut, stumbling over rocks and cursing his own lack of speed—not that it mattered. No man could have survived that explosion. When he reached Strobridge, the man was lying face down in the gravel. Darby gently turned him over and gaped. He *was* alive! And still conscious, although his face was badly lacerated.

Darby glanced up at the rim of the trench and saw curious faces. "Alert the doc!" he yelled. "Hurry, men!"

Darby's huge arms slid underneath Strobridge and he

picked the superintendent up as easily as a child. Then, with the bloodied face staring up at him, Darby began to run.

Perhaps Strobridge would live. His breathing was labored, but Darby couldn't see any sign that his throat or chest had been punctured by the rock shards. That was good, because the man's face was a sight and, even worse, one of his eyes was gone.

"The fuse—" Strobridge gasped.

"What . . ." the cut was an eight-hundred-foot trench and seemed like a mile. "What about it?" Darby panted.

"Tampered with!" Strobridge garbled. "Fuse tampered with!"

Darby wanted to ask him how, but they were both fighting for air and so a conversation was impossible.

"Hired!" Strobridge groaned as Darby staggered into the camp yelling for the doctor. "You're hired!"

"Thanks," the writer breathed as he handed the man over to outstretched hands.

Everyone in camp came running once the news was out that it was none other than Strobridge himself who'd been critically injured. Darby went unnoticed as time passed, while the doctor worked inside the infirmary car to keep his patient alive.

"Do you think he'll make it?" someone asked him.

Darby shook his head. "I don't see how he even survived the blast."

"Oh, God," someone swore. "He'd better die, or he'll return to hunt down the poor devil who messed up on the fuse setting."

'The hell with that!" another raved. "If he didn't drive everyone so damn hard, then things like this wouldn't happen all the time. We're tired! That causes mistakes."

"Sure. I know that. But not when they blow up in the boss's face!"

"Yeah, well I hope the sonofabitch is already dead. If he comes back, I say we should all quit!"

"I'll second that," another voice echoed. "Either we get a decent man to work for or I say we all walk off this accursed job."

There was a roar of support just as the coach door swung open and a grim-faced Charles Crocker stepped out on the boarding platform.

The roar died half-born and a thousand men grew silent and waited for the verdict.

"He's going to live," Crocker said quietly.

A low mutter of curses, though no man spoke openly.

"He's lost some vision. We've decided to take him to a Sacramento specialist. He'll be laid up for a while."

"How long, Mister Crocker!" someone hollered.

Crocker's face tightened. He knew how these men felt about Strobridge. "I don't know. A week. A month. A year. Maybe he won't be fit to come back ever!"

The mob glanced around at itself. Some smiled openly, the rest exercised more control. All of them seemed to take on new life.

"Who's going to take his place?"

Crocker blinked and it was easy to see he'd been too upset even to consider the accident in terms of his own railroad problems. That told Darby two things: in spite of his bluff and bluster, Crocker was compassionate and, secondly, even though he might not approve of Strobridge's handling of men, he liked his superintendent and was deeply shocked by this tragic mishap.

"I . . . I don't know," he admitted before them all. Then he seemed to realize he was in charge and had to put on a show of decisiveness.

"I'll appoint . . . I appoint Mister Philip Rait the Third as temporary superintendent while I'm in Sacramento."

This time the crowd shouted its approval. That is, everyone except one man.

And that was Darby Buckingham.

Chapter 5

Darby started to work the next morning and Philip Rait III made sure he had the toughest job on the line. The dime novelist could have protested, and quit until Crocker's return, but he didn't. Instead, Darby swung the sledgehammer, drilling blasting powder holes until his arms knotted in pain.

His unprotected hands quickly blistered and the salt sweat that ran into his eyes stung like blazes. But he kept swinging and vowed to see the day through no matter how badly he hurt.

At mid-morning, he'd been hammering for nearly four hours and it seemed like forever. He was wondering if he'd make it until the short lunch break when Rait called an unexpected ten minutes' rest.

All up and down the cut, men grinned hugely and began talking about how they'd finally gotten a boss who had some decency.

"Tired, mister?" Rait said, basking in the glow of his newfound popularity as he swaggered over to the prostrate writer.

"No sir," Darby answered, realizing he had to act subservient in front of the others.

"Good! In that case, I want you to start loading that pile of big rocks when the rest period is over. I'll have a crew of wheelbarrow handlers waiting."

Darby stared at the formidable mountain of oversized rocks, every one of which probably weighed at least a hundred pounds. The stack was twenty feet high and obviously had been accumulating for weeks.

"Thanks."

"Don't mention it." Rait grinned at some of the other workers. "You boys doing all right today?"

"Yes, sir! Mighty nice of you to give us a rest."

"Hell," Rait shrugged, "you fellas aren't animals and shouldn't be treated as such. That's why I'm extending the lunch break and calling mid-afternoon rest stops as well."

Their faces reflected their astonishment and pleasure.

Rait walked on down the cut, explaining that things were going to be different as long as he was in charge. He told this to a lot of men and, before he'd finished, the ten minutes had become thirty. Some of the workers even started looking nervous. One of them said, "Lucky old man Crocker took Strobridge into Sacramento last night to see that eye specialist. He probably won't return for a couple of days. But, when he does, Crocker is going to go wild when he sees what's going on here—or isn't going on. Sure as hell, that young fella is going to be axed. Ask me, I think we'd all be smarter to get up and get busy."

"What? And have everyone come down on us for suckin' up to management? Hell, no! Rait's the boss now and we'll never go back to the way it was under Strobridge."

The man rolled over toward Darby. "Say, stranger. What's that young fella got against you?"

Darby shrugged and rose to his feet. He didn't give a damn if the other workers liked it or not. They were going on forty minutes and that was stealing company time. "What's he got against me? Damned if I know," he growled, heading for the rock pile.

Darby's action signaled the end to the rest period and he was aware that several men shot him angry glances. A few minutes later, when he started to load the big rocks, they shoved their wheelbarrows at him impatiently, trying to push him hard. He ignored them and forced himself to work a steady pace that he figured would last him through the day.

As he lifted rock, he thought about how it was now going to be impossible for Strobridge to return as superintendent since Rait had been placed in charge. Darby agreed that the rest breaks were needed and the hours ought to be shortened. Tired men *did* make fatal errors. But, as he loaded one wheelbarrow after another, he noticed that the entire crew seemed to have slacked off. Men by the dozens were standing around talking or laughing, and those who worked really were just going through the motions.

The blasting almost came to a standstill and, for the rest

of the day and even though Strobridge had nearly finished the cut, the progress could have been measured in inches.

Rait called it quits an hour early, which probably saved Darby's life. He was so exhausted he could barely move, much less stoop and bend to lift another boulder.

The next morning, someone forgot to blow the locomotive whistle and the entire camp slept in an extra hour. Since the cooks had also overslept, breakfast was late and the morning shift didn't get underway until nearly eight. Even so, Rait and everyone else seemed in no particular hurry to make up for the lost time. At ten o'clock, Darby loaded another wheelbarrow, feeling the stiffness finally leaving his body. Then he heard the young superintendent shout, "Rest break! Ten minutes!"

The crews dropped their tools and grinned mightily. Working for the Central Pacific Railroad was starting to look better every minute!

At least it did until Charles Crocker and Harvey Strobridge, his face a mass of bandages, rolled up to the work site.

It happened during the afternoon rest break, which had been stretching on for more than twenty minutes. No one saw the carriage, but they sure heard Strobridge's outraged bellow.

"What the hell is going on!" he thundered, half stumbling, half falling out of the carriage and running, bent over double with pain, toward the top of Bloomer Cut.

Darby dropped the boulder and stared upward as the tall, wild man ripped the bandages from his face and shrieked, "Get to work, you lazy bums! To work, I say, or by all that's holy, I'll strip your worthless carcasses with a bullwhip and hang you all from a trestle!"

Charles Crocker, laboring under his ponderous weight, came to a stop beside his foreman in time to see half the crew still rising to its feet. His eyes sparked fire as his withering gaze swept over the crew and surveyed the absence of any progress these past two days.

"Damn you, but Mister Strobridge has my support! We leave for thirty-six hours and *everything* stops. Rait! Where are you!"

Philip reluctantly appeared from behind a piece of machinery and squared his shoulders. "Here, sir. I was just . . ."

"Just nothing, young man! Get out of there and wait in my coach, for I have words that only you should hear."

The young man colored deeply. One minute ago, he'd been the center of attention, everyone's friend. But now he stood in humiliation, stripped of respect, shorn of his fleeting authority. And watching him, Darby saw the embarrassment change to naked hatred.

"Yes, sir!" he lashed.

Strobridge threw his bandages down in fury. "All right," he ordered, "because you've all been on a holiday with pay, you're going to have to make up for lost time. That means I'll have lanterns set up before daylight and after dark for the next few days. You *will* get back on schedule and lay track through this granite rock in two days, or I'll cut your pay!"

A massive Irishman, fierce-looking and with a battle-scarred face, swore, "The hell you say! Me and the boys are going on strike!"

Darby thought Strobridge was going to leap into the trench, and that sixty-foot plunge would have killed the superintendent for certain, even if he were fit to whip the towering Irishman.

"Damn you, Clancy O'Brien! You and the rest of your boys aren't going to strike, because you're *fired!*"

Clancy's lips drew back from his horse-shaped teeth. "You can't fire us when we're strikin'!"

"How can you strike, O'Brien, when I'm coming down to tear you apart!"

Clancy blinked. He glanced at his supporters. Then he yelled, "Come on with you, sir, and I'll finish what the black powder should have done!"

There was a furious struggle on top as Crocker grabbed his half-crazed superintendent and kept him from flying into the long trench. Had the railroad president not weighed 265 pounds or more, he'd never have been able to handle the lighter man, because Strobridge almost went insane with the need to take on Clancy O'Brien and his friends.

When Crocker finally managed to summon help and drag his man away from the rim. Darby shook his head in wonder. Harvey Strobridge sure as the devil wasn't a bluffer or back-downish. He was tough as nails and had the heart of a lion, if perhaps the brain of a rabbit.

Now, as the workers began throwing down their tools in strike and walking over to offer sympathies to Philip Rait,

Darby knew that Strobridge, in all his dedication and zeal, had just made a serious mistake. He'd pushed far too hard. Young Rait had the edge, because he was related to Crocker and realized he probably wouldn't be fired no matter what. But what of Strobridge? With the men on strike, he was out of a job.

Scores of men decided to quit outright and head for the promising Comstock and Virginia City. Darby tried to tell them he'd already been there and that all the good claims were staked. The Comstock wasn't placer mining where anyone with a gold pan and luck could strike it rich. Not at all. Rather, it was deep rock mining, hot fetid air and disastrous cave-ins. No one listened. Those who didn't quit on the spot and demand their wages were going on strike. One way or the other, the Central Pacific Railroad was a dead duck.

Sometime late that night, Darby heard the crunch of a boot near his face. Remembering how a stranger had come upon him only a few nights ago with the intent of slitting his throat, Darby lashed out and clamped onto the foot, then yanked it viciously.

There was a surprised grunt, then a loud gasp as the man crashed to the earth. "All right," Darby gritted, clamping his hands around the man's gullet, "What do you want?"

There was a gurgling sound as the fellow's mouth opened and closed like a land bound fish.

Darby squeezed harder. "Who sent you! What's behind this!"

"Crocker," came the tortured squeak. "Crocker sent me!"

"Oh." He released his stranglehold. "You should have said so earlier."

Darby left the poor fellow fighting for air and probably wondering if his windpipe was collapsed.

When Crocker opened the door to his coach, Darby entered quickly and with certainty that he'd not been observed.

"Thank you for coming," Crocker said. "I know the risks you're subjecting yourself to. But . . . well, as you might imagine, Mister Strobridge and I are greatly concerned about this strike business. We thought, having worked with them, you might have a better idea how to handle this mess."

"What he wants to know, Mister Buckingham, is if they're serious or just bluffing."

Darby looked at Strobridge. His face was badly torn and someone had rebandaged his missing eye. "They're not bluffing," he said quietly.

"Damn!" Strobridge exclaimed. He peered at the writer. "I lost my temper out there today. If I . . . if I apologized, took back what I said about working extra hours, would that end this thing?"

"You'd do that?" Darby was surprised. He'd underestimated Strobridge's commitment to the railroad and now realized that it transcended his own pride.

"Yes, I would."

"I'm sorry, but it's too late to make amends. I listened to them all evening and they've really whipped themselves up to a fever pitch on this strike."

"Damn that Clancy O'Brien!" Strobridge raged. "I'll beat the life out of his Irish hide and then fire him and his friends."

"You'd only make things worse," Darby said pointedly. "Besides, with your facial wounds and eye injury, it would be suicide."

"Of course it would," Crocker interrupted. "Harvey, you've had your say and it's caused us serious trouble. I want a cool-headed opinion and that's why I've summoned Mister Buckingham out of his bed at this hour."

"You'll have to wait out the strike," Darby said.

"Never!" This time it was Crocker who yelled. "If we give in to their threats now, we're liable to be blackmailed every mile of the way."

"Maybe we could use that newfangled European blasting oil they call nitroglycerin," Strobridge offered. "I've heard it's eight times as powerful as black powder!"

"Uh-uh," Crocker grunted with a definite shake of his head. "A couple of months ago, the damn stuff leveled half a block in downtown San Francisco. I read about it. Seems a Wells Fargo agent, not realizing what it was, tossed it in their back lot. Killed twelve people and shook the ground for miles. Made everyone so scared they've outlawed all shipments of nitroglycerin from entering California. It's too unstable. Hell, it could blow half our crew to smithereens!"

The excitement in Strobridge's eye died. "Well then, we're whipped."

"Maybe not," Darby said quietly. "I have an idea."

"Then spit it out, Mister Buckingham! We are desperate."

"Hire Chinese."

"What!" two voices echoed. "Preposterous!"

"Why?" Darby challenged. "On my way over here, I met a group of about fifty of them. I was temporarily disabled and forced to stay in their camp a few days. They're extraordinarily industrious."

Strobridge looked at his boss. "Sir, Mister Buckingham's idea to employ coolies is well-intended but highly impractical."

"Why?" Crocker asked, looking up suddenly.

"Because our regular crews wouldn't stand for working on the same project with them Celestials."

"Give me another reason," Crocker demanded shortly. "I just said I would not be blackmailed."

"All right! The most blackimportant reason is that we could never feed 'em. If Buckingham was their guest, he'll tell you they eat the most outlandish fodder you ever heard of. Won't touch beef, nor beans or sourdough bread, boiled potatoes or coffee. Hell no, they won't. Drink sweet tea from little cups like women, they do."

"Their food isn't that bad," Darby argued.

"Oh yeah, well that's *your* opinion and one that not many whites would share. But the main thing is there's no way the Central Pacific could keep those little yellow monkeys in cuttlefish, bamboo shoots, mushrooms, rice, seaweed and whatever else they eat."

Crocker frowned, and glanced at Darby.

"I'd suggest," the writer said with unconcealed irritation at the open prejudices of the man, "that you hire them under the agreement that they buy and prepare their own food. They'd want to anyway."

"I wouldn't pay them extra," Crocker said.

"You wouldn't have to," Darby replied pointedly. "They're nearly starving. Just don't exploit them."

"What do you care?" Strobridge asked brusquely.

Darby thought of the heavy gold medallion under his shirt and how it had saved his life.

"My reasons are my own."

"Don't matter." The railroad superintendent pivoted to Crocker. "Sir, if what I've said up to now still ain't enough, think about how damn puny they are. Why, eatin' nothing but fish and greens and rice gives those yellow midgets no strength at all. None of them are physically strong enough to do a man's work like we require here in moving earth and stone."

Darby, remembering the weight he'd lifted these past few days, was inclined to agree but decided to remain silent.

Crocker lit a cigar and studied the smoke for a few moments before answering. "What you say may well be true, Mister Strobridge, but something keeps contradicting the line of reasoning that they can't do heavy work."

"What does?"

Crocker exhaled. "They built the Great Wall of China, didn't they? Biggest goddamn piece of masonry in the world!"

Strobridge's mouth dropped open and then shut tight. He was beaten for the moment and knew it.

Crocker made his decision and turned to the writer. "Do you think you could find those Chinamen you mentioned and bring 'em here with the understanding that, if they don't work, they're out the end of the first day?"

"I'll gladly try."

"Good. But tell them there may be real trouble from the main crew. They're going to hate the Chinese who come in here busting up their strike."

"Can you protect them?"

Crocker's eyes fell away but his voice was flat and tinged with bitterness. "Hell no, I can't. I'll try, but if a thousand white men riot, no one could save fifty Chinese. You tell them exactly how it is, Mister Buckingham. Just the same way I told you in the letter."

"Very well. When should I go?"

Crocker glanced at his pocket watch. "It'll be daylight in an hour. We've just enough time to kill a good bottle of brandy."

Darby smiled grimly. "That's an excellent suggestion. I think this is going to be another very long day."

Even Strobridge smiled. "Maybe. Maybe not. It all depends on how my little talk goes with Clancy O'Brien. Someone rigged that fuse knowing I'd be the last to go. I'll start by asking Clancy."

Darby stared at the man. He still hadn't figured out the construction superintendent. Headstrong, courageous or just crazy? Well, it didn't matter. In another hour, he'd be on his way back to the south fork of the American River to ask Chen Yun and his men to return with him.

In a way, he hoped they would refuse. Because if they didn't, and their arrival touched off a riot, then he, Darby Buckingham, would be responsible. There was no question now about sabotage but, next to the prospect of a strike-busting race riot, even sabotage seemed insignificant. This entire thing could erupt into mass butchery.

Chapter 6

Chen Yun studied each of his countrymen before turning back to Darby Buckingham. "We are ready."

"Good. Just follow me and pretend you don't understand a word of English. If there's any violence, I'll be the one responsible for ending it quickly."

Darby took a deep, calming breath and started down the hillside with the Chinamen behind. Since leaving, he could see that the Central Pacific hadn't moved an inch because of the strike.

Fifty small men. Could they make a difference? Maybe. There was the real possibility that they'd break the strike if they weren't beaten or killed. And, if they proved capable of the brutal work, then Crocker would hire others. Thousands of others. Up until now, he'd been unable to recruit and retain more than a tenth of the manpower needed to beat the Sierras.

Darby shook his head. He was getting way ahead of himself and, as they trooped forward, he heard a shout of alarm and saw the indolent army rise to its feet and then, slowly, come to realize the threat.

Big Clancy O'Brien and a dozen more almost his size came to the fore and then hundreds of men came flooding out of the camps toward Darby and the fifty Chinese. He could feel his pulse racing and imagined that Chen Yun and his countrymen must be terrified.

"Don't let them run," Darby warned. "If they do, we're dead men."

Chen Yun spoke quietly over his thin shoulder and with remarkable calm. Finished, he said in English, "They will stand by you. Die, if necessary. But this they believe will not happen, for they feel your strength."

Darby swallowed drily, then riveted his total concentration on Clancy O'Brien. Sometimes, if one could take out the leader of the opposition, swiftly and convincingly, it was possible to scatter the foe.

"You, Mister! Come not a step further!"

Darby didn't check his forward stride a whit.

"I mean it!" Clancy roared. "There is a strike going on here and we'll not be toleratin' those yellow heathens."

"Is that final?"

"Damn right. And the others stand fair and strong behind me."

Darby took one more step, planted his left foot down hard and unleashed a booming overhand right that exploded against the Irishman's jaw and slammed him down flat on his backside.

"Get up!"

Clancy shook the fog out of his eyes. He tried to gather his feet up under his body and finally managed to wobble erect. When he raised his fists, Darby bore into him, driving two more punches to the body and flattening him for keeps.

"All right," he demanded. "Who's next!"

No one moved. They just stared at Clancy as though they couldn't believe their eyes.

"These Chinese are staying and they've been hired to do a job—your job. Anyone who thinks different can quit."

Darby spun around and motioned for the Chinese to come forward.

"Look out!" a voice yelled.

Darby twisted and two gunshots split the air. A bullet blistered meanly past his ear and then he heard a low cry and saw a body strike the ground.

Harvey Strobridge grasped the smoking rifle in his fists and marched forward with Charles Crocker. "Anyone else care to pull a gun?"

No one answered.

Strobridge used the toe of his boot to roll the body over. "Who knows this man?"

There was no answer.

"Rait! Did you hire him in my absence?"

Philip came down to examine the still figure. "No."

"Damn good thing," Strobridge snapped. He gazed at the sea of faces and Darby noticed he was squeezing the rifle's stock so tightly his knuckles showed white.

"It's time we had ourselves a meeting," he said, glancing toward Crocker, who nodded for him to go ahead.

"All right, listen up. To begin with, these coolies are here to do jobs none of you seem to want. You know what I'm talking about—the menial things like moving rocks and filling dump carts. We've hired them because you people think you're too good for that kind of work."

Clancy stood and pointed accusingly at Darby. "You caught me with a sucker punch, mister. It won't be the same next time."

"Don't bet on it, my friend."

Clancy ignored him. "Mister Strobridge, me and the boys won't work beside those people."

"You won't have to. I'll keep you apart. If they cut it here, they've happily agreed to work for thirty dollars a month and they'll feed themselves. You people get thirty-five plus board and the better jobs. Is that agreeable?"

"What if it isn't," someone in the crowd yelled.

"Then you're still fired," Crocker shouted. "You've got the best of it and you'd be smart to accept."

"Not if he's going to drive us like animals," Clancy said tightly. "We'll be taking a morning and afternoon break—ten minutes and no more."

Strobridge's face contorted with anger.

"Give it to them," Darby stated flatly.

"He's right," Crocker added.

"Okay. Ten minutes, but not a second beyond."

Clancy glanced back with triumph and pressed for more. "And no working by the lanterns, like you swore we'd have to do."

Strobridge shuddered with inward rage, yet he nodded.

The Irishman relaxed and pivoted. "Well, you all heard him, lads. I say we end this strike and show everyone that no coolies can keep up with us. What do you say? Are you with me?"

There was a general murmur of assent and, almost as one, the Central Pacific crew started back to their jobs.

"Mister?" Clancy asked.

Darby turned.

"Who the devil are you? I never been hit like that before."

What the hell, Darby thought, there was no use pretend

ing any longer. Not after the stance he'd first taken. "Just between you and me?"

"Sure! On my dear Mother's grave, it's our secret."

"All right then, my name's Darby Buckingham."

Clancy slapped his thigh with a crack of his huge right hand. "The Derby Man you'd be called!" He massaged his jaw. "I might have guessed. It's . . . it's been a pleasure to be tapped by you. Maybe some fine Saturday night we might share a cup of whiskey and have another go of it?"

"Of course."

"Good then! And I'll be glad to be gettin' back to work then and showing up those little friends of yours."

"You can try," Darby replied, "but if I were you, Mister O'Brien, I wouldn't be betting my wages on the outcome."

The powerful Irishman winked. "We'll see. We'll just see."

And see they did. Even Darby was surprised at the way the Chinese took to the job. Chen Yun kept relaying Strobridge's orders to them and they moved almost at a run in their eagerness to comply. By the end of that first day, they'd cleaned out all the dump piles and carted the fill to a nearby ravine.

"I never seen anything like it," Strobridge was heard to mutter over and over while, on the other side of the roadbed and up ahead, the regular crews were anything but delighted.

On the second day, Strobridge decided to gamble and he gave Chen Yun the order to start driving the dump carts. The Chinese accomplished this with such skill he was astounded, although Darby tried to explain that these men were used to harnessing and driving animals, being from agricultural provinces.

"Well, they sure as hell have surprised all of us," Strobridge admitted, "but it would bust 'em to do the heavy work."

"Such as?"

"Such as using a pick or swinging a hammer as I understand you tried all one morning."

Darby winced at the memory; his hands were still sore, though he'd insisted on working with the main crew in order to head off any kind of trouble.

"Test them," Darby said.

"Maybe I will. Chen Yun, come on over here."

"Yes, one-eyed bossy man?"

Strobridge actually grinned. For some reason the description amused him. "Go down to the supply tent and break out a dozen picks and hammers."

Chen Yun bowed and was gone. But, later that night, when his men neatly stacked their tools, Strobridge was a believer.

"Is there anything they won't tackle?"

"Yes," Darby said smugly. "Beef, beans and coffee."

"Who cares? I don't even object to 'em drinking tea while they work anymore."

"Why should you? The Central Pacific isn't paying for that either."

That first week was both an agony of the body and an ecstacy of the spirit for the dime novelist. Though he labored side by side with Clancy O'Brien, the crews were suspicious of him for the role he'd taken that first day with the Chinese. They didn't trust him, yet their animosity eroded a little each day as he worked right along with them, neither asking nor giving any special favors. He lost twenty pounds the first month and his normal smooth roundness vanished into the sharp contour of power and muscle. When he swung a hammer, his twenty-two-inch biceps were an awesome sight and there wasn't a man among them who wanted to challenge him.

At night, Darby slept in their camp, although he occasionally stole away to Crocker's railroad coach for a nip or two of first class whiskey. It was just one such night, when returning to his blankets, that Clancy stepped out of the darkness and called him aside.

"There's trouble abrewin', Derby Man."

"Go on."

"I've heard talk that some scoundrels are fixin' to run out the Chinese tomorrow night."

"But why! They've done their work."

"Too well, I think."

"Can't you talk them out of it?"

"No," came the answer. "My boys number only a few hundred of the total. The others go their own way and keep private council, though when it comes to something like facing up to Strobridge, they're quiet enough."

"Then we'll just have to try to stop them." He peered up at the Irishman. "Will you help?"

"I'll think about it. The boys have a suspicion that Strobridge intends to hire more coolies. Is that true?"

There was no sense trying to deny it. In just a few weeks, the Chinese had proven their worth at any task. Strobridge and Crocker were enthusiastic and planning to hire as many as they could lure out of San Francisco and the Sierra gold camps.

"There'll always be plenty of work for you and the others who want it," Darby replied. "You know as well as I do that we're in a race with the Union Pacific and that this company is scraping every dime it can get to stay in contention. That's why Strobridge and Crocker push so hard. Besides, we're behind schedule and haven't even come to the steep places."

Clancy snorted good humoredly. "You already sound like one of them, Derby Man."

"Look," Darby explained patiently. "It's not a matter of the workers or management. It's a matter of this company's *survival!* If the Chinese are beaten and run off, this railroad is likely to fold. Then you and all of your friends will be out of work."

Clancy's look of amusement was gone now. "I hadn't thought of it that way."

"Well, you'd better, and tell the others, too."

Darby twisted his mustache with indecision. Up to now, he hadn't a clue as to who might be behind the sabotage and Strobridge's near-fatal accident. He needed help and he trusted his judgment enough to know that this simple, straightforward Irishman hadn't a devious bone in his huge body.

"Clancy, there's a group of men who are trying to ruin the Central Pacific by sabotage."

"Come on with you!"

"No, I'm serious. All those accidents? They weren't accidents. They were deliberate, and that includes Strobridge's."

"Are you certain?"

"Yes. Do you have any idea who is behind it?"

"Hell, no! A strike is one thing, but killing innocent working men is another."

"True." Darby frowned. "It's quite likely that the ringleaders behind this idea to run off the Chinese are also the saboteurs. Do you know their identities?"

Clancy shook his head. "Everything is very hush-hush. The way I understand it, they're supposed to put on masks and gather around midnight with guns and clubs. Since there's only fifty Chinese, there won't be much of a fight."

"Oh, yes, there will be," Darby swore. "Tell your men to stay out of it. And one more favor."

"Asking is free."

"Try to find out the names of whoever is behind tomorrow night's attack."

"I will."

Darby waited for a quarter of an hour until he was certain no one would connect the two of them, then he headed for camp.

But he didn't sleep much that night. Instead, he lay awake, gazing up at the constellations. Most people called the Chinese "Celestials." Funny, that meant someone or something connected with the heavens. Well, if he, Strobridge and Crocker didn't come up with some kind of plan, fifty Chinamen would be winging their way to heaven by this time tomorrow night.

"Are you certain, Mister Buckingham?"

"Yes," Darby said to the railroad president.

"It might be a blessing in disguise," Crocker mused. "If we can capture the leaders, I think it's safe to assume we've eliminated our opposition."

"Unless," Philip Rait said carefully, "such men do not exist. We still have no proof."

"Proof!" Strobridge shouted. "There's no eye behind this patch I'm wearing! How much more proof do you need boy?"

Rait colored deeply. His lips were tight and bloodless "Perhaps, had you exercised more caution . . ."

"Gentlemen! Stop it this instant," Crocker ordered harshly. "We have very few hours to come up with a plan and I'll not waste them with arguments."

Darby approved. He'd thought Strobridge and young Rait were going to start swinging and this wasn't the time for division.

"As I said, there is a chance that Clancy O'Brien may

decide to help. Also, he's going to ask around and see if he can find out exactly who's behind this."

"Good man," Crocker grunted. "Harvey, see he gets a ten-dollar-a-month raise. That's dangerous business."

"Yes, sir."

"And send a telegram to the U. S. Army post at Sacramento. Tell them we'll need a detachment to meet us just over the east ridge at sundown. That ought to give us plenty of time to set up for those villainous devils!"

Philip Rait headed for the telegraph that was rigged up to the third coach.

Crocker grinned at Darby. "Take it easy, Mister Buckingham. I've got a feeling your pal Clancy will put the finger on the men we've been seeking. Just think, after tonight, it will all be over."

Darby nodded. "I hope so. But I won't sleep easy until the threat is past."

"By midnight," Crocker promised. "We'll have 'em by midnight."

He was wrong. They waited past midnight, then until almost five in the morning for the attack, but it never came. When the first tinges of color glowed off the eastern Sierra summits, everyone was angry, bleary-eyed and irritable from the long hours of rigid concealment.

"You and the troops may return to your post, Lieutenant," Crocker said shortly. "It appears we have been hoaxed. Thank you for coming."

He pivoted to Darby, and it was an effort for the man to speak civilly. "Please tell Clancy O'Brien to come to my office immediately. He'll be picking up his wages—for good!"

Darby headed back for the camp. In a few moments, the locomotive whistle would sound and then he'd have trouble finding the Irishman.

"Get up, Clancy!" he yelled at the sleeping figure. "You've got some tall explaining to do!"

But Clancy didn't move and, when Darby threw off the big Irishman's blanket, he saw why. A knife was buried to the hilt in Clancy O'Brien's great chest.

Darby sank down to his knees as he was engulfed in wave after wave of bitterness. The Irishman had gotten into something even bigger than himself and had died for his trouble.

"I'm sorry," Darby choked. "I guess you did find out their names—as I *swear* I will some day!"

Then, he pulled the blanket over Clancy's still face. When he rose to his feet, there was a black fury in his expression that would make the devil himself shudder.

Chapter 7

My dear Miss Beavers:

I must begin by apologizing for the long delay in writing. I have been working very hard during the day with the construction crews, and at night making notes for my next story about the building of this great Central Pacific Railroad. If, indeed, it will be built. But, I'm getting ahead of myself.

More and more, the story itself concerns the Chinese, the conflict between races, and the ever-present reality that we are being sabotaged. Mister Strobridge and I have both nearly been murdered on several occasions. Despite everything, I cannot discover who is behind this villainous plot. I know only that they are bright, well-informed and totally ruthless. Accidents and death continue almost weekly.

We must push ever higher toward Donner Pass Summit but are now blocked by Cape Horn. It is but fifty-seven miles out from Sacramento and consists of a mountainous cliff which rises almost straight up over the American River. Mister Strobridge estimates the height over water to be nearly one thousand feet and the Cape itself descends at an angle of at least seventy-five degrees. Not even a goat could stand on its surface. Yet, we must tear a ledge up its great wall and lay track.

The American crews have refused to work on Cape Horn and I do not blame them. The Chinese

(Crocker's Pets, as they are now being called by everyone) are willing to assault this massive stone buttress. There are now several thousand of them in our employ as Mister Crocker, after emptying the streets of San Francisco's Chinatown, has now begun to recruit them directly from China. It is expected that many more thousands will come before we beat the Sierras. I sincerely hope they do not arrive to perish at Cape Horn.

Tomorrow, Chen Yun and his men will begin the deadly work above the American River. Do not worry, my dear. Nothing in heaven or earth could get me into one of those flimsy reed baskets. My job will be to try to negate the vulnerability of our crew during this assault on Cape Horn. I will write again, sooner this time. Until then, my love.

Sincerely,
Darby Buckingham

"Are they ready?" Darby asked Chen Yun, as he eyed the flimsy baskets with unconcealed skepticism. It didn't seem possible the latticework of Sacramento River reeds could hold one Chinaman, let alone several.

Chen Yun spoke briefly with his men, then pivoted back. "They are ready, Derby Man. I have instructed them carefully."

"All right." Darby could feel the eyes of the American crew on them all as he stood beside the cliff and tasted the wind and spray rising off the river far, far below. The Chinese had spent only one afternoon weaving the three waist-high baskets into which they'd knotted four eyelets, in the directions of the Four Winds, and inscribed them with the proper prayers. New ropes were tied through the eyelets and now they were ready to be lowered over the side. Big snubbing posts were planted deep in the rock and four men each were responsible for playing the human cargo down the cliff's rough face.

Darby peered down at Strobridge and Crocker, who were at the bottom of the cliff and gave the signal, "Lower the baskets!"

Chen Yun repeated the order to the twelve strongest Chinese in camp. Then, the baskets disappeared over the cliff's edge and there was nothing to be heard except the wind and the raw grating of rope and wood.

Darby watched dry-mouthed as the baskets descended jerkily, foot by terrifying foot. A sharp gust of wind tossed them sideways.

"Hold it!" he shouted.

For a moment, nothing moved. Not the Chinese huddled together over empty space nor those above who grasped the ropes. The gust passed, leaving everyone shaking. "All right," he gritted, "continue lowering."

Chen Yun repeated the orders and the baskets inched downward.

Strobridge relayed hand signals to Darby, indicating where each of the baskets was to stop and the tedious and frightening work to begin. And now, as Darby positioned each of the baskets along the cliff's face, he motioned downward to the watchful Chinese. His signal was accepted and, in the swaying baskets, the Chinese began to pound away at the rock wall with their hammers.

An hour later, it was with great relief that Darby gave the order for the baskets to be raised. The Chinese had managed to drill and light the long black powder fuses. One by one, the baskets were brought up and, as the last one edged precariously over the lip to safety, a loud roar of approval went up from the American crew.

Chen Yun and the Chinese workers smiled at the accolade. Then, they bowed deeply. Witnessing this moment, Darby felt a real surge of hope and knew the Chinese would no longer have to endure torment and ridicule by the Americans—they had finally won their long overdue respect.

As if in salute, the charges exploded across the cliff wall and tons of rock blossomed out into the air and showered the American River. Through the smoke and dust, the writer laughed openly to see Strobridge and Crocker locked arm to arm, doing what was obviously a spontaneous jig beside the roaring river.

Over the next few weeks, Crocker took most of the American crews past Cape Horn to grade roadbed and build trestles over the increasingly numerous ravines. Darby stayed with the Chinese at Cape Horn and supervised the blasting from above while Strobridge signaled from below.

The superintendent's mood had become almost ebullient.

His spirits soared as the Chinese progressed rapidly across what had so recently appeared to be an impossible fortress of stone. No one, not even Darby, could have anticipated how the little men took to the work. Perhaps it was because of their natural love of fireworks, for they actually competed to see which basketload of powder monkeys could set the longest simultaneous explosion. This required great precision in cutting the fuses so that each would fire its drill hole charge just one instant after the next.

Cape Horn shook with rolling thunder as both Strobridge and Darby marveled at the skill and daring of these men who now only required to be raised from the blast by the scantiest distances. And, so far, not one coolie had died. It seemed incredible.

"You forget," Chen Yun told him one afternoon, "that the Chinese have a long history of building roads up cliffs such as these. Have you ever seen our famous painting of Emperor Hsuan tsung's retreat from his Tang Dynasty capital in 775 A.D.?"

"No."

"You should, for it contains a cliff even greater than this one with a winding road up its face supported by logs. This famous road existed for centuries like a stairway to the heavens."

Darby moved over to the rim. It seemed impossible that a road could be supported by hanging logs, but he had no doubt it was true. Thankfully, and because of the slight angle to the rock face, the Central Pacific track would be cut into the wall and there was no danger of it ever collapsing—or so the engineers promised.

Strobridge gave the familiar signal and Darby ordered the fuses to be lit and the three baskets raised. He was pivoting toward Chen Yun when he heard the tortured sound of splintering wood from the nearest snubbing post. In one frozen moment, there was a loud crack; then the post flipped up into the air.

"Hang on!" he yelled. But his words were too late. Three of the four Chinese were whipped down and the last barely managed to cling to the lowering rope as the broken post furrowed its way toward the cliff's edge like a sharp plow blade through sandy soil.

Darby lunged at the post and tackled it a mere yard

before it would have sailed out into nothingness. But even his great strength was tested as the post jerked toward the edge; the Chinese howled from below.

"Chen Yun!" he cried and the man was instantly grabbing for the rope, digging in his heels. For a moment, it was the two Chinese and the writer struggling frantically to hold the suspended weight at all costs. Darby tried to root his heels, but the gravel shale offered no purchase as he scrambled and felt himself being pulled inexorably closer.

Chen Yun wasn't doing any better than he was and, as they inched toward the lip, the first Chinaman had to release or he'd have gone over.

"Dig, Chen Yun! Dig!" he gritted, knowing the others couldn't help for they had their own baskets to raise or . . . or the black powder explosion would blow their dangling countrymen to pieces!

Far below, he heard the three men whose lives he held babbling in terror. And, even in that moment, as Darby's great muscles bulged and strained to hold the rope, the writer had the image of how they must feel, suspended a thousand feet over the American River with a massive charge of black powder about to explode just a few yards overhead.

Somehow, his heels found purchase only inches from the cliff's edge and, with every ounce of strength he possessed, gritting and straining until veins stood out in his face, he held them.

"Pull, Chen Yun! Pull or. . . ."

The warning was torn from his lips as the explosion rocketed upward along the cliff wall and blasted hot air and pulverized rock into the sky.

The weight in Darby's hand vanished. One moment he felt like he was supporting a mountain, the next, it was all gone. Darby flipped over backward as a cloud of grit floated down to bathe his sweating face. He didn't have to drag himself over to the edge and peer downward toward the ribbon of glistening water, because he knew he wouldn't see anything. The Chinese were gone; torn into a thousand bits and spinning along with the rock into the turbulent river so far below.

It was only later that evening, when he stood beside the cliff alone and gazed into the sunset that Darby blinked and his eyes suddenly grew hard and cold. The post! He hurried over to its buried base realizing that someone had covered it with dirt. Darby's fingers brushed the dirt away until the broken edge was visible.

And then he saw what he should have known from the first—it had been sawed three-quarters through right at ground level.

A rock turned behind him and Darby threw himself around into a crouch as he prepared to spring.

"So," Chen Yun said quietly, "my people also begin to feel the cold touch of death by murder."

"Yes, my friend. Now, we are all in danger. I have not been able to discover whoever is behind this, but I know the day will come when I can guarantee your safety. Until then . . ." his words trailed off. "Until then, there is still work to be finished here. Will your people go over again?"

"I do not know. Our agreement with Mister Crocker was that those of us who die are to be returned to China so that our spirits do not wander this foreign land crying in loneliness."

"It couldn't be helped," Darby said evenly. Both of them knew full well that the Chinese needed this job as much as the railroad needed them. "I'll . . . I'll ask Mister Crocker to post guards."

Chen Yun's face was wintry. "It is too late," he said sadly.

"But why!"

"Because, though they do not fear death so much, it is our belief that their bodies must be sent home to China and that those who died earlier are forever damned."

"I see."

"All right. Tell Crocker we will continue to build, but not go over this cliff again."

"He'll understand," Darby said wearily. "But there's still half a day's work left before we've cut all the way across. Tomorrow, I'm going over to finish the job."

Chen Yun studied his face. "Why? Does this railroad mean that much to you, Derby Man?"

He thought about it, looked out over Cape Horn to the west and saw the already lain tracks glistening redly in the sunset like a pair of bloody claw marks.

"Yes," he whispered. "I hadn't realized it until now, but I guess maybe it does."

For long moments, they watched the day fade, then

turned toward camp. And, at the place where their trails separated, Chen Yun said, "Tomorrow, I will go with you. This I must do."

Because of Darby's extraordinary weight, Strobridge and Crocker double-rigged the ropes to both the snubbing posts, which had been yanked out, inspected and reset. The two remaining baskets were placed one inside the other to give them extra strength. Crocker insisted on a dozen Chinese to lower them, one handhold at a time.

"Are you certain you want to go?"

"Yes," Darby said tightly. "Let's go while I still have the stomach for this job." He paused. "One more thing."

Crocker's expression was tight and the strain showed in his eyes. "Name it."

"Keep your rifles up and at the ready. If someone does open fire, we've got no place to hide."

Strobridge swore. "Dammit. *I* should be the one going over the side, not you!"

Darby knew it wasn't an empty gesture intended to ease the man's conscience. "We've been through all that, Harvey. You're indispensible here and going over in that basket would be a clear invitation for attack. Since I appear to pose no great threat to them, perhaps this will be blissfully uneventful."

"It better be," Crocker vowed. "I've got a dozen riflemen scattered along the rim. If anyone tries to potshot you, they'll be riddled."

"Good," Darby said, trying to force a smile. "I just hope *they* realize that."

He stepped into the suspended reed basket and felt the fiber crunch ominously underfoot and the damned thing sway. Darby almost got sick for a moment as his eyes dropped. And maybe he'd have leapt out of the basket, realizing the madness of his gesture, if Chen Yun hadn't climbed in beside him.

"Lower away," Darby croaked as he squeezed his eyes tightly shut and gripped the suspending ropes. Dear God, he thought, as the basket started bumping its way down, what have I done?

When he was in position, he signaled those high above to stop lowering. Darby inspected the work with an uneasy stomach but an appreciative eye. The roadbed was blasted almost across the entire face of Cape Horn and was plenty wide and safe enough for men to complete on foot. Once this last stretch of ten yards or so was completed, these flimsy reed baskets could be discarded. A gust of wind rocked them and Darby felt sweat popping out all over his body. He was eager as hell to be done with this and back up on top.

"Over some more!" he yelled, craning his neck up at Strobridge and hand-motioning them forward. "Another three yards!"

The basket dragged across rock and dislodging pebbles, which spun for what seemed to be minutes before the stones splashed into the distant river. "Hold it!"

As they'd rehearsed that morning, Chen Yun selected a drill and leaned far out of the basket. Darby began to hammer. It was torturous work. He was off balance and, each time his weight shifted or another gust slammed into them, the writer felt his heart seize up like a block of ice. What made it even more difficult was trying to make certain his hammer struck the drill and not Chen Yun's fist.

They set five charges in holes two inches deep and spaced a foot apart. Next, while Darby tamped the holes full of black powder, Chen Yun carefully measured the fuse lengths so that they'd all explode together with maximum impact.

"Are you ready to light?"

Chen Yun nodded vigorously and, as Darby glanced upward, he noticed that the sun had traveled a good forty-five degrees across the horizon. They'd been at work nearly four hours.

"Go ahead. As soon as they're burning, I'll give the signal."

Chen Yun's hand was as steady as the rock itself when he began to light the fuses which had been carefully selected from a long coil and then inspected for tampering.

The fuses caught instantly and spluttered with smoke and white-hot light. When the fifth one took off, Darby yelled, "Take us up!"

As if in response, a heavy caliber rifle thundered over the river and its big slug tore straight up, ripping through the basket's floor.

"Look out!" Darby shouted, reeling off balance as another shot slammed in between his feet, shattering reeds in its wake.

From topside came frantic yells, then they heard Crocker's guards open fire. But they were shooting blindly down into the spray and shadows. And their rifles sounded like Chinese firecrackers compared to the boom of the ambusher's weapon.

Like a fist, the next slug punched up between his legs and tore a ragged gash of flesh and reed across the inside of Darby's calf before it hummed meanly away.

"Take us up!" he roared.

One of Crocker's men seemed to spot the rifleman and edged way out over the rim to fire. The hidden rifle thundered again and it was so loud that Darby knew it had to be a heavy buffalo rifle, the kind that would throw a fifty-caliber slug a mile. It sounded like a Ballard or a Remington Buffalo Gun. Whatever it was, the man using it was fast and knew the smaller rifles above were overmatched. So, when Crocker's sharpshooter leaned out, the buffalo rifle plucked him off the wall and pitched him downward into a long, screaming dive.

Darby's head was thrown back. What in the hell were they doing? "Get us out of here!" But, even as he felt the rope jerk, he knew it was too late. The marksman below was long overdue to score a hit on either Chen Yun or himself, and Darby could feel the floor of their basket starting to buckle.

It just wasn't going to wash. And, in one awful second, he could see only three alternatives, each of which was fatal because they'd either get shot, blasted off the cliff face like yesterday's Chinamen or the miserable reeds underfoot were going to separate enough to open like a death funnel.

It seemed like a hell of a way to go, any way it happened. Darby heard Chen Yun cry out in pain as a slug tore up into his leg. The writer grabbed for his friend and, for a split second, they almost toppled out of the collapsing basket.

Darby held Chen Yun erect and stared at the five sizzling fuses. Already, they were nearly gone. Darby gnashed his teeth in helpless defiance—they didn't have a Chinaman's chance.

Chapter 8

O^r did they?

A Buckingham never gave in, no matter how desperate the odds. Darby snarled, then measured the distance to the ledge. Damn! Too far. If he'd had a running jump at it—or even been able to push off on solid ground—he might have the slimmest of chances, but never from the lip of this wretched basket.

What then! Think, Man.

The fuses. Now that he was dead certain the basket would never be pulled up in time, he *had* to get those fuses. Darby reached out until his entire upper body was exposed to the rifleman below and he snatched them one by burning one with his bare hands and hurled them into the rising mist. The buffalo rifle thundered and a slug tore through the flesh under Darby's arm. No matter. With grim satisfaction, he threw the last stubby fuse down at his assailant. "Blast you!" he shouted.

One of his feet dropped through the basket, pitching him sideways to its floor. His fists closed on the supply of fuses and black powder still ready for use and, at that very same instant, he knew a breath of hope.

"Hang on, Chen Yun!" he shouted as he tore off his belt and wound it loosely around the half-filled sack of powder. "I'm going to drop a bomb!"

He snatched up the roll of fuse, ripped off a foot of it and looked down at the wounded Chinaman. "How long?"

"One finger."

"Are you certain?" Darby exclaimed. As fast as these fuses burned, he was half afraid it might explode in their faces.

Chen Yun's knife flashed and Darby crammed the fuse

into the sack, leaving no more than an inch to hang. Then, he cinched the belt tight and, with his feet braced wide to keep from falling through, he struck a match and cupped it out of the wind. "There she goes!"

A bullet plucked his sleeve as he took aim and pitched the bomb into a long, arching fall. He watched it trail smoke into the rising spray.

There were at least thirty pounds of black powder and, when it exploded, a pillar of rock and water geysered hundreds of feet into the sky. Darby saw it sprout upward, higher and higher toward them and, with a yelp, he grabbed Chen Yun with one hand and the four connecting overhead ropes with the other as the blast hit the deteriorating reed basket and flung it against the cliff as if it were a bird's nest in a hurricane.

They were smashed into the wall and, the next thing Darby knew, both he and Chen Yun were lying in the cut staring up at the azure, cloudless sky. The writer eased himself into a sitting position and peered down at the American River.

A big black cloud of smoke was floating over the white water. He saw an uprooted tree going along, too. Other than that—nothing but blasted rock and leveled underbrush. The big rifle and the marksman who'd used it simply were no more.

After the two had been roped and pulled up to safety, Crocker sort of collapsed beside them. The railroad president fumbled into his coat pocket and brought out cigars. His fingers shook badly as he poked one into each of their mouths and struck a match.

"Well, Derby Man," he said raggedly, "you blew the rifleman all to hell, but you and Chen Yun didn't do a thing to that rock wall. Guess you're going to have to go back over and finish what you started."

Darby gaped at Charles Crocker.

"Don't take it so hard, big fella, there won't be anything to it this time, you already got the holes drilled."

Darby inhaled deeply. "Mister Crocker, like the wise Chinese, I know when I've had enough. From now on, I'm going to keep my feet planted on solid ground, thank you. And I'm redoubling my efforts to discover who is behind this."

"Well," Crocker said slowly, "I don't think you're going to get any clues from down in that gorge. Whoever it was got himself painted all over the rocks."

Darby scowled. The man was right.

Crocker examined his cigar. "I'm going to have a hell of a time getting anyone to finish the job. Got any ideas?"

"No, but don't waste anyone of value." He turned. "Maybe there is someone who'd do it for money and glory."

"Who?"

"Your nephew, Philip Rait the Third."

"Hmmm," Crocker mused, blowing smoke. "This time you just might have something. Whoever is trying to cripple the Central Pacific Railroad sure wouldn't want to put that man out of action."

It was meant as a joke, but Darby Buckingham didn't laugh, because it was his opinion that truer words had never been spoken.

Wesley Bryant was the chief purchasing officer for the Central Pacific Railroad and worked out of both its San Francisco and Sacramento offices. He seemed perfectly suited to be the assistant to Charles Crocker's partners, Huntington and Hopkins.

At thirty-eight years of age, Bryant possessed a definite air of self-importance gained from years of valued service. He had earned the right to spend tens of thousands of dollars for construction equipment with just a nod of his head. A shrewd bargainer, he was reluctantly admired by the many he'd bested in financial dealings.

Unknown to his conservative employers, he was also admired by sporting men and women for his ice-cold nerves in a brawl or card game. He was a professional and a loner by nature. If anyone thought about him, it was usually with a mixture of awe and dislike. Wesley Bryant was a taker and an opportunist—he was also brilliant in a cunning and deadly way.

By the very nature of his job, he was never in one place long and, at least once a week, he visited the construction site in order to determine the Central Pacific's future requirements. If, for example, rails were to be ordered, his buying decisions would be made almost eight months in advance of delivery so that he could telegraph his counterpart in New York and the best prices might be obtained.

Now, however, buying considerations were the farthest thing from Bryant's mind as he dismounted and checked to be certain that Strobridge and Crocker were out on the job. Satisfied, he opened the telegrapher's door and slipped inside.

"Hard at work, I see. You and our special friend must have it all under control."

Jack Gibbon jerked in his chair and the week-old Sacramento Union slipped to the floor.

"Well, hello, Mister Bryant, we wasn't expecting you so early this week."

"Obviously not. I came because I was told our great Central Pacific Railroad overcame Cape Horn last week. This was contrary to my expectations. Tell me, Gibbon," he said very softly, "is it true we are marching forward again?"

Gibbon's head bobbed and his Adam's apple yo-yoed.

"Yeah, but . . . but we tried."

"Tried?" A crack appeared in his voice as it rose. "Tried! I was assured that this railroad would winter at the base of Cape Horn!"

"Now, wait a minute," Gibbon pleaded. "You know I'm not responsible. I just do as I'm told."

"Get him," Bryant hissed. "Track him down and bring him to me, now!"

Gibbon bolted through the door and Bryant began to pace back and forth in the small, littered office. He was, he decided, going to have to take over at this end, find a pretense to spend more and more time in camp. With Cape Horn beaten, Strobridge could now drive his crews right through Sailor's Spur, Emigrant Gap and Cisco, straight for Donner Pass. Dammit anyway! There was no more room for mistakes. This railroad must be stopped.

Footsteps sounded quickly on the railcar's wooden steps, then a bluff but guilt edged voice said with a hollow ring, "Well, hello, Wes, Jack and I thought sure you were. . . ."

The half-finished sentence was smashed as the visitor pivoted and lashed out with a wicked backhand squarely into the face of Philip Rait the Third.

The younger man gasped in shock and pain, then dug for his gun. He might as well have taken the time to comb his hair first, because Wesley Bryant's hand streaked down and his gun was cocked and leveled before Rait could quite believe his eyes.

"Don't die for your foolishness," he warned.

"You can't kill me," Rait whispered. "If you do, everyone will find out you've embezzled company stocks to buy that lumber company."

Wesley Bryant laughed, but it was a cold and deadly sound. He cocked the hammer of his gun back and, out of the side of his mouth, he drawled, "Gibbon, choose up now. You gonna live . . . or die with this fool?"

The telegrapher didn't even have to think about it. "I'm with you. We can say he committed suicide because his uncle shamed him. And . . ."

"No!" Rait cried, his eyes flooding with terror. "I . . . I didn't mean it, Wes. Give me another chance. PLEASE!"

He made the fool sweat for almost a full minute before he gently let the hammer down and holstered his gun. "All right, one more time. One more chance, Philip. Now, you tell me exactly what went wrong this time. Then, I want to know what your future plans are—if you do indeed have a future."

Just ten minutes later, they were through. All he'd heard were excuses and he'd had his fill of them for months. "To begin with," he gritted, "we've got to eliminate Darby Buckingham before he decides to write to some newspaper about what's going on."

"But how?" Rait cried. "We've tried to kill him three times—once even before he arrived, I waited to shoot him into the river. Another time, when Lee went out to stab him and, yesterday, in the basket. What else are we supposed to do?"

"Succeed, dammit!"

He leveled his finger at the subdued pair. "And I'll tell you something else. The Panama Steamer Lines and the California-Nevada Stage Company have paid us a lot of money for results—not excuses. And I'm sure as hell not going to see my new holdings go under."

Rait said bitterly, "That's where the real money is—and it's all yours, Wes."

"You didn't complain when we made our deal. You boys looking for an out?"

"Uh-uh!" Gibbon croaked, realizing full well the only "out" was a plot in the cemetery.

"What about you, Philip?"

"No. But it still galls us that we've only received a few thousand so far for all the risks we've taken."

"And failed at," he corrected icily. "The trouble is you

aren't following through on anything. Buckingham was beaten up but now he's fine. You rigged a fuse and Strobridge lost *one* eye—not both or his life. You almost had a strike but even that failed."

"We've delayed things," Rait groused. "Because of us, this railroad is weeks behind schedule."

"That's nothing! I want it stopped. Dead. Busted. No more."

Bryant realized he was losing control and that wasn't his style at all. He ran his fingers through his wavy brown hair and said, "Listen, this railroad is on the very brink of financial disaster. My boss, Collis Huntington, spent the last six months in New York and Boston and he could unload no better than $150,000 in Central Pacific bonds, even giving his own personal guarantee for the interest."

"That won't last long."

"Of course it won't. But the man is not about to quit—none of them are—because they've sunk everything into this operation. Now, Huntington has just finished paying two politicians over ten thousand dollars to teach him the art of lobbying before Congress. He's on his way back to Washington."

"He'll fail," Rait said. "I handle the books, remember? We are way over budget and hopelessly behind schedule. And it'll get worse with every mile. Strobridge can't beat Donner Pass."

"That's what you said about Cape Horn," Bryant snapped. "And if we'd stopped him there, they'd have laughed him off Capitol Hill. Now ... dammit, I just can't say."

"What happens when he can't even reach the summit?" Gibbon asked. "Man, the snows get forty feet deep up there. Those little coolies will freeze."

"They'd better," Bryant vowed. "Something has to happen. I want Collis Huntington to receive a telegram upon arrival in Washington that the Central Pacific Railroad has just suffered another major setback."

For the first time, Philip Rait smiled. "Wes, you've got almost as much to lose as the Big Four."

"What do you mean?"

"Just what I said. I understand how the Panama steamship line and the stage will go under if the transcontinental goes through, but I'm not sure where you stand."

Because he was very sure of himself and very vain, Bryant said, "All right, it's like this. When Congress approved the Railroad Act, Crocker, Huntington, Stanford and Hopkins for the Central Pacific and Doctor Thomas Durant of the Union Pacific won their concessions on the platform of service to Americans. But what they really want is to make money by hauling freight *as well* as passengers."

"Makes sense."

"Sure it does," Bryant agreed. "They'll wait a year or so, then go full scale into the freight business."

Rait's eyes widened. "And what could be more lucrative than timber?"

"Correct," Bryant said tightly. "And, since their train goes right over the Sierras, they'll log it like crazy. It's a perfect set-up to haul lumber down the mountains to Sacramento and San Francisco."

"And drive your newly acquired Alaskan logging operation right into bankruptcy."

"Yes. But I knew that when I bought it and that's why the previous owners almost gave it to me. You see, up to now, the Sitka Logging Company could ship timber down the Pacific Coast far cheaper than it could be hauled by wagon down from these mountains."

"How much can you sell?"

"As many board feet as I can stack above and below decks. Sacramento and San Francisco are booming. It's a nice profit and, if you succeed here, I'm willing to cut you both in for a handsome piece."

"What about the ice?"

He'd neglected to tell them that, but it did add considerably to his fortune. "It covers my operating expenses."

"Sure it does!" Rait crowed. "Everyone in San Francisco knows you load up the forward holds of your ships with ice from the glacier near Juneau, then pack it down with sawdust from your lumber mill. In summer, a man has to pay nearly double for ice in his drink and that adds up to a lot of money you'll lose if the Central Pacific also starts hauling ice down from Donner Pass."

Bryant shrugged. "All right," he admitted easily. "No one ever said we were playing for small change. So, we agree that we all stand to profit hugely if we can stop this railroad. Now that we've gone over the stakes in this game, I hope you both understand why we must not fail."

"Easy for you to say," Gibbon whined, "but Strobridge and Buckingham are both on guard now. Crocker keeps a couple of gunmen near each of 'em during working hours, though I don't think they know it."

Bryant scowled. For long moments, he wrapped himself in silence as his nimble brain sought a solution. Then, all at once, it came and he snapped his fingers. "I've got it!"

"What?"

"Listen, forget about Buckingham and Strobridge for a couple of weeks. I've just had an idea that can't miss!"

He glanced at Rait. "Tell me again about that Chinaman who speaks English."

"You mean Chen Yun?"

"I mean the one who went over the side of the cliff with Buckingham. The head coolie, dammit!"

"Well, not much to say. He takes the orders in English and translates to the Chinese. Seems to be their leader."

"Hmmm," Bryant mused, "do any of the other coolies speak English?"

"Not that . . . say, I'm beginning to follow you now! You want us to kill him and . . ."

"No. Crocker has Chinese recruiters in San Francisco who contract for overseas labor. He'd just hire one of them and we'd be right back with the same old problems."

"Then what?" Rait's expression reflected his confusion.

Bryant leaned closer, trying to keep the excitement in his voice from being too obvious. "I've a better idea. One that will shut the Central Pacific down once and for all."

An hour later, he stood up to go. "Crocker wants me to inventory some things today so I'd better get to work. Tomorrow, he'll send me back to San Francisco to reorder, but I'll return in no more than ten days. Is that sufficient time for you to hire some new men and carry out my plan?"

"Sure," Rait exclaimed confidently, "but it's going to take some big money."

Bryant threw down a roll of bills. "There's another five thousand. When I return, this railroad had better be dead in the water—if you follow my meaning. Succeed and I'll have ten thousand more for each of you. Fail and . . ." He left the warning unfinished, to dangle ominously.

Rait and Gibbon looked at each other and it was the first one who said, "We won't fail this time."

Bryant allowed himself to smile. "I don't see how you can. It's simple and will be totally unexpected. When it happens, there's not a damn thing Crocker, Strobridge *or* Buckingham can do to save the Central Pacific."

He carefully placed his Stetson on his head at just the proper angle. "Time to go to work, gentlemen. When I return in ten days, we'll have a private little celebration."

"Yeah," Gibbon said, with the glow of dollar signs still bright in his eyes.

Wesley Bryant left then, with a good feeling that this time they *would* prevail. Yes sir, he thought, a little cunning and a lot of money were an unbeatable combination.

Chapter 9

C hen Yun followed the Chief Surveyor through the pines, traveling higher and higher. The air was sharp, indicating that, at nearly six thousand feet, winter was approaching.

He shivered as they topped an exposed ridge and a blast of icy wind streaked down off Donner Pass. It reminded him that he must ask his friend Darby Buckingham to see about ordering winter clothing for his people. He'd already delayed the request too long. Not only were heavier coats needed for the thousands who already were employed, but the thousands more who would be arriving to work on the Central Pacific would be needing them as well. Recruited by labor contractors, the immigrants usually were advanced passage money—forty dollars if they came by fast steamship and twenty-five if by sail. They repaid it with interest from their railroad wages. Given the exorbitant interest rates, it usually took three or four months for them to pay it back, during which time they also had to purchase food and this new, heavy winter clothing.

The Chinese spokesman was worried. So far, accidents and sickness had claimed less than two dozen of his people but, in the high mountain passes, the dangers would be far greater.

"Say, Chen Yun, that's the ravine I wanted you to see. We've measured it and the damn thing is four hundred and twenty feet across and nearly eighty feet deep."

Chen Yun waited. This was a case where they might decide either way—trestle or earthen embankment.

"I think I'll recommend to Crocker that we bring in seven or eight hundred of your coolies and start digging into the slope over there. You can haul fill dirt after I lay in drain pipe at the base. How long will it take?"

75

Chen Yun thought about it very carefully. They'd already faced ravines such as this, but none quite so vast. With seven or eight hundred men, plus a few hundred horse-drawn dump carts. . . .

"Two weeks, Mister Wilson."

The chief surveyor frowned. "I was afraid you'd say that. Mister Strobridge is going to raise a fit when I tell him about this one. All he can think about is that first tunnel."

Chen Yun said nothing. Though he and Mister Wilson had often taken these reconnaissance surveys to study impending labor needs, Wilson made it clear he regarded the Chinese as physically and mentally inferior. Chen Yun understood this, but it didn't particularly concern him, except when prejudice manifested itself as ill treatment or violence. Wilson was not the kind to do either.

"I ain't even going to tell Strobridge about the trestle you people will have to build at Deep Gulch," the surveyor mumbled to himself, obviously dreading any news he had to relate which would cost either time or money. More and more, Chen Yun thought, these obstacles were presenting themselves as they neared Donner Pass. One didn't have to be an educated American to see that things were going to get far worse before they topped the Sierras. For instance, there were all those tunnels.

"What do you prefer, trestles or the earthen embankments?"

The Chinaman shrugged inoffensively. Now that he'd seen what the next task would be, he wanted to return to camp and order those clothes. He was freezing in his light cotton shirt! Would Fing Yi be able to leave for San Francisco? They could all. . . .

"You people really don't give a damn what you work on as long as your bellies are full of rice and you can send home some American money to Mama San. Ain't that right?"

"Yes, Mister Wilson," he said, trying to smile but realizing his face was numb and he'd failed.

"Ah, hell, don't give me that look. I got nothing against you coolies. Sure, you've taken a lot of jobs from white folks, but then you've earned respect since Cape Horn."

Wilson buttoned up the collar of his heavy sheepskin coat, then toed the damp pine needles. "Are you going back to old China when this is over?"

Chen Yun was startled by the question because it was personal and also something he hadn't really considered. Never to return to China was frightening—like cutting away part of his body. Yet, America was young and free. Even for the Chinese, there was unheard of opportunity.

"I hope to stay."

Wilson glanced at him, worry creasing his broad forehead. "Sure hope all of you don't feel that way. Hell, there's more than five thousand of you now and Crocker is planning to double that figure by year's end. You won't believe the tunnel we have to bore under Donner Pass."

Chen Yun wished this man would stop talking. The temperature was plunging and, up through the canopy of trees, he could see huge dark clouds with tongues of fire striking downward into the forest. Up above, just another thousand feet, there was a blizzard raging and the invisible barrier of warm camp air was evaporating, leaving the Central Pacific vulnerable.

"Yeah, before you people see the sunshine again, I got a feeling a lot of you are going to pack your little teacups, get back on those ships and sail home to China."

"Perhaps, Mr. Wilson, we had better return to camp."

"Sure, but there's one thing I've got to ask. And I mean no harm. Fact is, Mister Rait and I were discussing it just yesterday, and when I told him we were coming out here together to see this job, he made me promise to ask."

"What is it," Chen Yun said quietly.

"How do you coolies do without any women so long? Does that opium sorta make it easy?"

Chen Yun flushed deeply, turned away in anger and shame. And, though he feared a lashing, his words could not be held back. "It works," he said, "for some of us, just as the whiskey does for some of you, Mister Wilson. Only, the next morning, we are not sick."

There was a long pause. "Reckon we'd best get on back to camp, Chinaman."

Chen Yun nodded and fell in behind as they picked their way through the heavy forest and piles of rock. They had been walking silently for about ten minutes when Wilson leaned against a boulder to catch his breath and suddenly yelled, "Look out!"

The Chinaman spun around as a fist crashed between his eyes and he felt his nose snap as he reeled in pain.

"Get him! Wilson is finished."

Through tears, he saw one of the attackers leap forward. Chen Yun moved backwards, then tripped and started rolling crazily down the mountain, completely out of control. He heard gunfire, then careened through a clump of Manzanita and skidded to rest at the base of a Ponderosa Pine.

Still half-dazed, Chen Yun felt the sting of bark as lead slapped it into his face. He didn't need anything else to clear his head and, at once, he was on his feet and running. He splashed through a leaf-covered stream and ran on and on until the voices and gunfire grew dim and his own breath burned his lungs. When his legs were shooting pain and too weak to control, he collapsed in the underbrush like a frightened and pursued animal. Only then did he realize that the water from the stream and his own sweat were beginning to freeze on his body and that it had begun to snow.

His benumbed mind whirled as he tried to figure out what to do now. Wilson was dead and the killers were searching for him. And he knew they would not stop, because he could identify at least one of them. He was one of Wilson's assistants, a tall, rangy young man named Metz. And the other? This made Chen Yun shiver, for he thought surely it was Crocker's telegraph operator.

Lost and freezing, Chen Yun cleaned his broken nose with a handful of fresh snow and headed down the mountain. His brain told him to *run*—to Sacramento, San Francisco, then China. But he couldn't. It would be a shameful thing and his people would call him a coward, and the Derby Man might even be murdered.

Chen Yun took a breath through his mouth because his nose was packed with dried blood. He, a coolie, must return to the Central Pacific camp and tell his friend that Metz and perhaps the telegraph operator were guilty. To do any less would be dishonorable.

Darby heard Cletus Metz begin to shout a mile from camp. Everyone, even the diligent Chinese, halted work and listened to the unmistakable tone of alarm in Metz's voice. And then, as the tall, wild-eyed surveyor burst into the clearing and sprinted down the roadbed, his voice rang clearly.

"It's Mister Wilson! He's been stabbed to death by a Chinaman! I saw him run away!"

Both white and Chinese crews dropped their tools and started forward. Darby was out in front.

"What Chinaman?" he demanded.

"Chen Yun. The one who can speak English."

"Impossible!"

Metz rocked back. "Mister, he's got a Chinaman's knife under his ribs and I watched it happen. I was going to ask Mister Wilson about how he needed a grade and I saw 'em through the trees. They were arguing and then all of a sudden that yellow devil pulled out his knife and killed Mister Wilson! When he realized I was there, he got scared and ran."

"Why didn't you shoot him!" someone demanded angrily. "Christ, Metz, you're packing a gun!"

"Too many trees. I tried, but there wasn't a clear shot. And you know what shape they're in. Hell, they can run up these mountains. No way I was going to catch him."

"You're lying!" Darby said with outrage. "Chen Yun wouldn't take anyone's life except in self-defense."

"Easy to say," Crocker said, puffing up to listen. "I know how you feel about Chen Yun, but there's been a killing and Metz is a witness."

"I'll tell you something," Darby said evenly. "If this thing stands on Metz's word alone, those Chinese are going to walk away from this railroad and never come back because they know, *and I know,* that Chen Yun is innocent. My God, Crocker, can't you see what's behind this!"

A bearded tracklayer snarled, "What the hell is going on? Mister Wilson was stabbed by one of these yellow bastard's frog stickers and we're just standing around talking!"

"We don't know for certain who. . . ."

"The hell you say, Mister Crocker! Metz here is an eyewitness. What more do we need to stretch the Chinaman's neck?"

Darby grabbed a pick. There was no mistaking his intent. "Anyone who tries to hang Chen Yun is going to have to deal with me!"

"You can't get away with this!"

"I'm not trying to 'get away' with anything!" he swore.

"Just give me five minutes alone with Metz here. I'll get the truth."

"Oh no!" Metz cried. "I seen you lift a rail all by yourself and I ain't about to dance your dance, mister."

"Leave him alone," Crocker ordered. "I'll not have him beaten."

"Then," Darby said, "you are missing the opportunity we've all been waiting for."

"Why . . . what do you mean?"

"To find out who's behind the sabotage of this railroad!"

That shook Crocker.

"What the hell is he talking about?" another worker shouted. "Wilson's been murdered by a Chink and. . . ."

"Look! There he is!"

Chen Yun, as small and vulnerable-looking as a child, stood on a great pile of fill dirt and then started down.

The crowd surged, but Strobridge grabbed a rifle and froze them with a burst of fire and yelled, "Everyone, stop! We hear this man out now."

Darby slammed through the crowd to meet his friend.

"I didn't kill Mister Wilson," he told them all.

"He's lying," Metz roared. "I saw him use his frog sticker. Saw him plain as day!"

Chen Yun's skin was almost blue with cold when he pulled up his shirt and brought out the six inch knife.

"That's it! That's the one he used," Metz shouted triumphantly.

"Is that the murder weapon?" Darby asked.

Chen Yun nodded, then reached back under his shirt and brought out the knife Darby knew to be his own. It had a bone handle with intricate engravings on it and one of them was the same lion and serpent depicted on his golden medallion.

"That," Darby shouted, "is Chen Yun's weapon!"

"No. That's not true!" Metz hollered.

Chen Yun gazed out at the cluster of accusing faces. Then, he placed the tip of his own weapon over his heart and looked beyond at the sea of Chinese. His head lifted and a shout rose in his throat as he cut his tunic with the knife. "Chen Yun. Sinong!"

Eight thousand Celestials nodded vigorously.

He pitched his knife at Crocker's feet and clutched the

murder weapon. Then, with a slicing rip that made Crocker gasp, he cut the blade across his chest again, drawing blood.

"Damn!" the railroad president whispered.

Chen Yun's expression did not change. Not even when he lifted the wet blade and held it up for all to see.

"Chen Yun," he called, pumping the murder weapon against the sky. "Chen Yun. Sinwai!"

Even in Chinese, there was no mistaking the high pitched roar of repudiation which lifted from their throats. Chen Yun and his knife were definitely from the Sinong Province of China while the murder weapon was not.

"Well?" Darby whispered, "are you convinced or do you think he actually rehearsed those thousands of men?"

Crocker shook his head. "I apologize, Chen Yun."

"Me too," Strobridge interrupted. "I'm ashamed, after what you've done. Now, can you tell us who really killed Wilson?"

"Yes." Chen Yun started to revolve and, in that instant, Metz snatched Chen Yun's knife from the ground and poked it against Crocker's overhung belly.

"Freeze or I'll kill him!"

No one moved. It had happened so quickly everyone was caught off guard. Everyone, that is, except a tall figure wearing a white Stetson hat who rode unobserved from the pine trees. His eyes were pale green, his face chiseled slate. Without so much as the blinking of an eye, he drew and fired and Metz went down with a bullet in the back.

"Jesus!" Strobridge gasped, looking up at the approaching horseman. "Did you have to kill him like that!"

"Yes," came the flat reply. "Mister Crocker, are you all right?"

The railroad president appeared shaken and in desperate need of a stiff drink and his next words confirmed the impression. "I am. And I owe you my life."

Wesley Bryant dismounted, strode past the gaping Philip Rait and heartily clapped his boss on the shoulder. "I do believe I'll accept your invitation, sir. I can't tell you how grateful I am to have arrived just in time to be of service!"

Crocker had insisted that Darby, Strobridge and even his young nephew, Philip Rait, join in on the party that evening. But, despite his relief that Chen Yun and Crocker had both narrowly avoided becoming fatalities, the writer was not in good spirits. It seemed, he thought bleakly, that he was never going to get any closer to the real saboteurs. Oh sure, they'd been lucky enough to blunder along and keep everything going, but it had been a very, very close call this day. If Chen Yun hadn't been smart enough to demonstrate his complete innocence so dramatically, things might have exploded, ending in the lynching of a brave and innocent man. Without question, that would have incensed the Celestials and driven them away, thus finishing the dream of President Lincoln.

These were his dark thoughts as he slipped outside to brood, and smoke, and watch the snow drift through the trees. Maybe Crocker and Strobridge hadn't quite grasped how nearly they'd come to being ruined this day. Later, they would and, like himself, they'd somberly realize that in the murder of poor Wilson, the ruse had been ruthless and diabolically brilliant.

"Mister Buckingham?"

"Ahh, Mister Wesley Bryant."

The man smiled and raised his glass in salute. "Don't tell me you're through for the evening. We've barely had a chance to visit and I'm told you are a man of many talents. Bare knuckles fighter, strongman, writer. Quite a list."

Darby shrugged his wide and sloping shoulders. "I work hard to keep my mind and body fit and ready to handle whatever may prove a test."

Bryant nodded and lit his own cigar. "Yes, I'm sure you do. That's why I wanted to ask privately, and man to man, what you think of all this business."

"What I think?" He didn't understand.

"Sure," Bryant urged. "You know. Being a novelist, you must have a feeling for intrigue and mystery. Perhaps be able to look at this with a professional eye. That's what Mister Crocker is counting on anyway."

"Did he tell you that?"

"In so many words. Are you denying it?"

"No."

The man waited. And waited. Finally, with a hint of annoyance creeping into his voice, Wesley Bryant said, "I gather you either don't wish to reveal your suspicions—or you're too embarrassed to admit you've come up with nothing."

Darby laughed, but his mustache twitched with disfavor. "Mister Bryant," he growled as he stepped into the night, "I'll leave that to *your* imagination. Good evening."

Bryant pitched his almost untouched cigar to a sizzling extinction and went back inside. His manner was as arrogant and distasteful to the writer as that of Philip Rait. But it didn't take much in the way of observation to realize that Wesley Bryant was twice Rait's equal.

"Derby Man!"

"Chen Yun! What are you doing out here at this hour?"

"I must tell you something. There were two men who attacked us today."

"Two?" Darby's pulse quickened. The obvious question was half-formed on his lips when the Chinaman spoke.

"I think the other was the telegraph operator."

"Jack Gibbon!"

"Yes."

"Tell me *exactly* what you saw."

When his friend was done, the writer clapped him on the shoulder. The account had convinced him that Chen Yun had probably been seeing quite well and there was every chance that Jack Gibbon was a saboteur. Maybe the *head* man!

"Do you think he knows you saw him?"

"I do not know."

Darby felt a nibbling worry. "If he does, he can't afford to let you live."

"I will be protected."

"From an ambusher's bullet?" He shook his head. "No, my friend, it's too risky. Until I get the truth out of him, you'll have to leave."

"But where?"

Darby scrubbed his jaw. "You know that abandoned miner's cabin up the line about five miles?"

"Yes. Mister Wilson and I passed it today."

"Good. Take some food. Go there early in the morning and wait for me. By tomorrow night, I'll know if Gibbon is mixed up in this or not and I'll have wrung the truth out of him."

Darby pulled his coat tightly about himself and shivered. "You know, as soon as I get you back, we're going to have to talk to Crocker about ordering some heavy clothes for your people. You'll never last through the winter the way you're dressed."

Chen Yun gritted his teeth against a chatter. "You are good to think of such kindnesses."

"You'd have thought of it yourself before the snow got too deep. I'll see you tomorrow night."

Blast! It was *really* cold! Darby watched Chen Yun disappear through the trees and enter his camp. Once among his own people, he was totally safe. The writer slapped his paws together for warmth and then froze at what he saw. "Gibbon!"

"Yes. One little sound and you're a dead man."

The telegraph operator stood covered with snow and the man's lips were almost purple. It didn't take much guesswork to figure he'd probably been waiting for hours.

"If you kill me, Chen Yun will tell Crocker," Darby warned.

"Tell him what? That he *thinks* he saw me? Hell, that don't worry me even a little. Now, keep your hands up and move."

"Where?"

"The roadbed, of course. And, beyond it, up to that cabin where your friend is going to be joining us in the morning."

"Why?"

The gun cocked. "You're asking too damn many questions. Let's just say I think it would be nice to give that little snipe a real surprise welcome. Now move or I shoot. Lower your hands below the shoulders and I pull the trigger. Understand?"

Darby indicated he did. Only one thing was certain— he'd never live to see Chen Yun arrive at daybreak and the Chinaman wouldn't survive much longer. But Gibbon would. He'd be back pounding the telegraph key before Crocker finished his after-breakfast cigar. And no one would ever suspect he'd murdered twice in less than eight hours.

No one at all.

Chapter 10

The snow had stopped falling and the temperature was near freezing. Above, the clear stars glimmered with detached brilliance while below his feet crunched on crusted ice. He had no trouble following the broad roadbed the first couple of miles. It was flat and smooth, made by thousands of Chinese who daily swarmed like ants, shoveling, wheeling hand or single horse-drawn dump carts, drilling, blasting . . . laboring. The road was a silvery ribbon through the emerald trees.

Darby said, "I don't suppose you would consider switching your alliance to a higher bidder?"

"You mean sell out?"

"Exactly. I am worth far more to you alive than dead."

"Probably, but my partners wouldn't see it that way. I'd not live to enjoy your money."

Darby halted, started to lower his hands. If he could get the man to. . . .

Gibbon said, "Keep moving or I'll shoot."

"Blast!"

"What?"

"Nothing." He searched for a way to reach Gibbon. "I was just thinking that, if you told us who's really behind all of this, you wouldn't have to fear retaliation."

"Don't make me laugh. If you, Crocker and Strobridge had any idea of who and what you're up against. . . ."

"Yes?"

"Never mind," Gibbon said abruptly. "Damn, it's cold! Move faster!"

The roadbed scraped over a hill and the wind hit them in the face with fresh driven snow. Just ahead, Darby saw a half-finished trestle in the moon-glancing snowlight. It was eerie, this skeleton of wood which spanned the ravine.

"Are we going to cross or hike down and out of this?"

Gibbon motioned him up to the edge. "Will it support us?"

"Of course. But it's only two feet wide and covered with ice."

"If you slip, I'll know enough to come back. Don't try anything funny or it's all over for you. In this damned wind, no one would hear my gun. I'd just toss you over and you'd not be found until next spring."

Unfortunately, Gibbon was right. There was a stream far below, but it was snow-covered and the ravine was soft and contoured with drifts. Yet, as the writer stepped onto the bridge, he knew time was running out. The cabin rested just past the next rise of land and that was where he'd be killed.

So, it was on this high, half-finished latticework of frozen timber that he was to compete for his existence. Because Gibbon was staying a good ten feet behind with the gun trained on his spine, Darby realized his options were precious few and, as he crept forward on the slippery trestle, he examined them.

First and most obvious, he could simply jump and hope he survived. His black eyes surveyed the gorge. It appeared to be hundreds of feet deep. Even with the cushioning snow, he'd surely kill himself down there. Or he'd be crippled by the fall and be a clear target. Or he'd crash through the ice-covered stream and freeze in minutes.

Darby checked off the idea of leaping. But dammit, they were now halfway across! Think, man!

He heard Gibbon slip and grunt. Darby whirled, lost his footing and slipped. In one horrifying moment, he almost dropped and only just managed to catch himself by his armpits.

"Get up! Get up or I'll shoot!"

He hauled himself to his knees and stood shakily. "I'm doing my best," he graveled.

When they were both upright, Gibbon yelled into the wind. "Try it again and you're a dead man!"

So what? he thought. Don't try anything and I'm also finished. Darby's eyes were running and so was his nose as the wind grew stronger and he began to place his feet carefully before him. Another fifty yards and he was across.

Fifty yards. He measured the drop as he moved ahead. Lessening now to maybe forty, then thirty feet to the embankment below; then twenty, then ten, then—he jumped!

Jumped as gunfire slammed into the wind and was battered away. One of the bullets angled through his jacket and sliced a mean furrow across his chest just under the dented medallion. But he didn't care. Darby landed and began to snowball down the ravine. He heard more gunshots and Gibbon's angry shouts, but the sounds were dim because his face was layered with wet snow.

A tremendous jolt hammered through his body and pounded the wind from his lungs. He gasped in pain, cuffed the snow from his eyes and realized he'd rolled into one of the trestle footings. In one glance, he saw that it had probably saved him from hurtling over a thirty-foot drop into the snow-covered stream.

But now what? He could hear Gibbon clattering over the last few yards of trestle and knew the man was coming down after him; identity revealed, he had no other choice.

Darby's foot caught on something and he fell heavily. As he cursed and scrambled erect, he reached down and grabbed a long splintered board which had probably been discarded by the workmen. He recognized it for what it had been—a piece of scaffolding. It was a good ten feet long and a foot wide at the unbroken end. Darby hefted it for balance. He could hear Gibbon crunching through the snow to finish him. The writer lifted the board and held it spear-like over his shoulder as he pressed in behind the footing. The light was bad; he was plastered with snow and Gibbon was expecting to overrun him as he fled in terror.

Darby gritted his teeth and his neck sank a fraction as he gathered his weight.

Then, suddenly, the man was there, his breath vaporizing in the cold, his gun out in front of his body.

"Wh. . . ."

The words died in Gibbon's throat as Darby threw the board at him. Gibbon screamed. The pistol bucked, sending an errant bullet skyward. Gibbon pitched off the embankment, crashing through the snow-crusted water below.

Darby stood under the trestle for a full minute, listening to the wind howl above and hearing the faint gurgle of water. But then, where seconds before he'd watched the body's outline, a thin sheet of ice crystallized and knitted like a transparent scab. The human silhouette, and the gurgle which came from it . . . vanished.

Darby Buckingham sat in Charles Crocker's traveling office and listened while the president of the Central Pacific Railroad read aloud an excerpt from the Sacramento Union.

> *The railroad has finally passed Cisco, ninety-two miles east of our offices, and is in daily operation. It transports supplies, coolies and even sightseers to this altitude of 5,911 feet above the level of the sea—higher than that attained by any other railroad in America—perhaps even the world.*
>
> *However, Mister Charles Crocker and his able assistant, Mister Strobridge, have, as yet, nothing to celebrate. We have received reports from a very reliable source, a well-known western dime novelist, that there is actual sabotage being carried out on the line.*

"Why did you tell them, Mister Buckingham?"

"Because," he answered, "the deaths of Gibbon and Metz raised inquiries that could not be dismissed. Anyway, once I write my book, it's going to be a part of history."

Crocker frowned, "I hope this entire effort doesn't become just a footnote. Listen to this."

> *Even without the danger of saboteurs, the fate of the Union Pacific grows daily more precarious. Blizzards are already slowing progress and now Mssrs. Crocker and Strobridge have reached a point where the very mountains themselves stand in the way of progress. Twelve tunnels, varying in length from 800 to 1,650 feet, are currently under construction along the snow belt between Donner Pass and Grizzley Hill, just west of Cisco. The first two are each less than five hundred feet long. They have been completed and are timber-lined. The remainder are being worked day and night by eight thousand Chinese, who drill and blast into the mountains and never see the sun. Mister Strobridge, despite his loss of one eye, continues to drive his crews around the clock in three eight-hour shifts. It*

*is said that many coolies are dying due to overuse
and the elements.*

"Damn that lying reporter!" Strobridge bellowed. "Sure
the Chinese are dying; whites, too, but not from overwork.
It's accidents, pneumonia and the way they have to live in the
tunnels to keep from being buried by avalanches."

"Take it easy," Darby said. "I know this reporter and I'll
straighten him out quickly. We're aware you aren't abusing
your crews."

Strobridge sat down heavily. He looked twenty years
older than when Darby had first met him. It was this weather.
These damnable blizzards that kept raging down on them one
after another—endlessly!

Darby said, "Let me finish this piece and then we can all
weep and go back to work."

*Of all the great obstacles ever faced by man,
Summit Tunnel at Donner Pass is surely the greatest. This hellish brute measures 20 feet in diameter
through 1,659 feet of solid granite, is 7,032 feet
above sea level and only 124 feet below Donner
Pass. We believe it cannot be completed for years.
In the meantime, the rival Union Pacific Railroad is
marching into Wyoming at the rate of a mile per
day. Undoubtedly, the poor backers of the Central
Pacific Railroad are envious of their counterparts
and, facing Donner Pass, are writhing in abject
despair. On behalf of the Sacramento Union, we can
only offer our deepest sympathy.*

"Thanks one whole hell of a lot!" Crocker snarled, then
balled up the paper and hurled it into the open maws of his
furnace. "I guess we'd better get back to work before the
Union Pacific arrives and discovers us frozen in Tunnel
Number Ten. Let's go!"

During the weeks that followed, Darby, Crocker and
Strobridge drove themselves with renewed intensity. Winter
clothes were obtained for the Chinese who were now widely
dispersed to the various tunnels so that all ten were being
worked simultaneously.

Winter roared down upon them with a relentless, frozen

fury. The mountain became as slippery as an iceberg and twice as deadly. All work outside the tunnels was halted because the snow rendered construction impossible. But, crawling at a foot a day, thousands of workers labored inside the tunnels with pick, hammer and blasting powder. And, even though the stone walls were damp and forbidding, a man had only to step outside into the wintery winds being hurled off Donner Pass to know he wanted to get back inside his cheerless sanctuary.

Machine shops, storage sheds and living quarters were erected right at the western portals of the tunnels. None of these wooden structures were more than a dozen yards from the tunnel's opening but, still, during the endless blizzards, men became disoriented while traveling between them and froze. Ropes were slung between the tunnels and the buildings to prevent this kind of tragedy. And, as the snow piled ever deeper, the sheds and shacks became buried, causing a labyrinth of snow tunnels to come into existence. Their arched corridors were made wide enough to allow passage of horse sleds. The tunnels themselves were often several hundred feet long and ended at dump sites where the sleds could unload blasted tunnel rock. The ceilings had an unnerving way of constantly settling as more snow fell up on top, but when they did not cave in, the laborers grew bold enough to just scoop out additional headroom as needed. So it was that, from November on, the men of the Central Pacific became subterranean creatures who never saw the bleak, shivering sun.

Avalanches were a dreaded part of existence for everyone. And, once, a buried housing quarters was flattened by the new weight of a mountainside's plunging snow. Fortunately, most of the occupants of that building were on shift and fewer than ten died.

But, even as the Chinese and the tunnel borers prayed in their caverns for an end to the terrible winter, Crocker and Strobridge had to keep men outside and they suffered abominably. They were the teamsters and railroad operators who daily brought in food, supplies and materials so that the work could continue.

"It's damned lucky we have rails laid past Tunnel Number Four," Crocker said wearily, "or I don't know how those freighters could reach us."

Darby held a cup of coffee to his lips as they crouched

on the leeside of a hill. He knew that tunnel was at Red Spur, just two and a half miles above Cisco at an elevation of over six thousand feet. It seemed as if they'd beaten it out of the rock years ago, but it had been only weeks and they were now less than ten miles east of that point.

"Seven miles between there and Donner Pass," he said, "and it seems like a thousand."

"Sure it does. That's because it's mostly all underground. Dammit! I got a telegram from Huntington saying we've got to speed up if he's to wrestle another loan out of those Capitol Hill boys."

Darby shook his head. "You know we can't go any faster. Strobridge has crews working from both sides of every tunnel on this mountain."

"Maybe so, but Congress doesn't *care*. They want results and never mind that this is the worst winter in years. Twenty-three blizzards! Twenty-three and it isn't even January yet!"

"Take it easy," Darby said, offering the man a cigar. "I don't know much about Congress, but it doesn't seem likely they'd cut you off after all we've gone through."

"They might," Crocker said. "But, even if they don't, these mountains are killing us. Here we are mired down under tons of snow and going practically nowhere, while to the east Durant and his Irish crews are racing across the plains, gobbling up free land and easy government money. Hell! They're getting rich and we're going bankrupt."

Darby extracted a flask of brandy from under his heavy coat. "Here," he offered, "take a pull and relax. There's nothing we can do now except keep going as we are. At least we haven't been sabotaged for a while."

Crocker upended the bottle and it was like a transfusion of blood the way his face flooded with color. "Yeah, I'd sort of forgotten about them," he admitted. "But why should they bother right now? We're all buried under and going practically nowhere."

Darby took a pull himself and said nothing. It was nearly dusk and bitterly cold, yet the panorama was harshly beautiful. The tall mountain firs were heavy with snow and their tips leaned toward the dominating mountain summit which brooded in a breath of thunder clouds. And, from his vantage point, Darby could see the shadowed openings of six separate tunnels and the great fires which constantly burned to keep them open and which now glowed like angry cat's eyes. The only sounds that reached his ears were the sharpening of hammer on steel, and the heavy, rumbling blasts which shuddered inside the mountains.

"Here," Crocker said. "Finish it and let's go, before that wall of white beats us to camp."

Darby glanced up toward Donner Pass. He was not at all surprised to see blizzard number twenty-four.

The big storm struck just as they reached the Tunnel Number Eight Camp where they were staying. Crocker and Darby hurried into the portal and out of the teeth of the wind, and were brought up short by Philip Rait.

"Mister Crocker! We've been searching all over for you!"

The brandy-warmth in Darby's stomach turned sour. Something was very wrong.

"What is it now?" Crocker asked, visibly bracing himself.

"Trouble. Bad trouble down at the Butte Canyon Bridge just below Cisco."

"I know where the hell it is! What's wrong?"

Philip Rait's expression changed. Now there was almost a satisfaction that leapt into his eyes as he delivered his report. "It's our supply train. Seems it fell through the Butte Canyon Trestle—sir."

Crocker staggered. A moan escaped from his lips and he leaned against the rock wall for support.

"How bad?" Darby asked. "Did the entire supply train go through?"

"I don't really know," Rait answered coolly. "You'll have to see for yourselves. Wesley Bryant is down there and I've sent a man to get Strobridge. Other than that, there's not much left to do."

Crocker recovered and stepped to the entrance of the tunnel. He gazed out at the driving blizzard. Then, he raised one massive fist and cursed the storm, yelling "Damn you, I won't quit! You can't beat us—only kill us. But I won't quit!"

Darby grabbed Rait. "Get him to his office and make sure he gets drunk tonight and sleeps or he's going to kill himself."

"Yeah. What are you going to do?"

"I'll wait for Strobridge and then we'll gather enough of

Chen Yun's men to fix that trestle. If we can't get supplies up here in a few days, these camps will die."

A half-twist touched the corners of Rait's mouth where his mustache ended. "Hmmm," he mused out loud, "you know, I do believe you're right."

Darby would have flattened him, but he had his hands full trying to talk the exhausted railroad president into remaining in camp while he and Strobridge took over below. There was another reason he insisted Crocker remain, and that was so that all three of them weren't out together in the raging blizzard.

If he and Strobridge didn't make it to Butte Canyon, at least Crocker might carry on the fight. As Darby stuffed a cigar between his teeth and touched it with fire, he gazed out and thought there was every chance they'd not make it to the wrecked train.

And if they did, what could they accomplish? The trestle was nearly eighty feet high and four hundred long. And there was a *train* in the gorge below while above a blizzard raged.

A horizontal blast of snow veered into the tunnel, slapping his face like a frozen fist. His cigar sizzled and went dead. Darby hurled it at the shrieking whiteness.

"Madness!" he whispered. "This is madness!"

Chapter 11

The trip down to Butte Canyon trestle *was* madness that night. Darby and Strobridge strapped on snowshoes and plowed their way through massive drifts and frigid winds that gusted to seventy miles an hour as they buffeted the mountain. The pair managed to stay on line only because the tunnels were so close together. At each, they collapsed beside a fire and thawed their numb extremities. At Cisco Tunnel, they ordered every man who wasn't on shift to join them as they purposefully slogged the last mile and a half to the wreck. Darby and Strobridge were totally exhausted and the Chinese laborers were already risking frostbite when they staggered over a ridge and witnessed the carnage of Butte Canyon.

"My God!" Strobridge cried, his oath wind-driven from his purplish lips.

"Yes," Darby muttered, pulling a scarf tighter around his face and trying to yell through it. "At least the engine didn't pull *all* the cars over."

"Let's go!" Strobridge yelled. "But I can't see what the hell we can do in this weather."

"Nothing!" Darby shouted. "We must get inside or these men will freeze."

Strobridge pivoted back into the face of the icy wind. "Where?"

"In the cars."

"But the trestle may collapse!"

"I don't care. It's our only chance," Darby hollered. And it was. In one glance, he'd realized the magnitude of the train wreck and the hopelessness of trying to work in this storm. The locomotive was gone. Darby could see it already snow-covered outline down in the gorge and trailing in its wake, two or three cars which reminded him of lumps of bread dough. Yet, miraculously, he counted twelve train cars which had not plunged into the gaping hole in the trestle. The first was balanced precariously in the driving wind, anchored in place only by its coupling to the next car.

Darby motioned everyone forward and they battled their way down the ridge to a halt beside the last car. Strobridge pounded on the back door and it opened. "What happened?"

"Someone blew the bridge out from under the locomotive," the man yelled. "Engineer, coal tender and everyone in the first three cars died in the crash!"

"Did you investigate?"

"Not me. Mister Wesley Bryant and a couple of other guys are down there now."

"Where?" He and Darby both stared into the swirling snow. It seemed impossible anyone could be down there and alive in such weather.

"I don't know where they are."

Darby waved the Chinese forward and held up all ten fingers.

"Now wait a minute here! We can't take a bunch of coolies. There's barely enough room for us now."

"Then you'd better get the hell out," Strobridge shouted. " 'Cause these men are coming inside. They're Crocker's pets and he sure ain't going to have them freeze!"

Darby grinned and, in doing so, split his lip painfully. No matter. It was good to see how the Superintendent of Construction had altered his feelings about these Chinese ever since they'd beaten Cape Horn. And, from his attitude as they quartered the Chinese in car after car, Darby had the feeling that if it came down to the unhappy railroadmen or the Celestials, Strobridge would choose the latter.

The last three cars nearest the chasm of splintered timber were abandoned because it was possible that additional sections of trestle might collapse at any time. Even so, Darby and Strobridge pushed up to the gap and stared across to the far side.

"Never seen anything like it," Strobridge whispered in awe and shock.

"And I hope you never do again," Darby replied, moving forward until he was huddled behind the tilted car and out of the wind. "I was foolish enough to hope they'd given up.

Harvey, we've got to discover who's behind this. If they'll send those railroadmen plunging to their deaths, they'll stop at nothing."

"I know. But that's *your* job. Mine is to clear these tracks and repair the trestle. Fast."

It was true. Darby slammed his glove against the wall of the teetering coach and swore in helpless frustration. Every time he thought that perhaps he had a lead—it vanished. And, when he had narrowly escaped ambush, the attacker himself had been killed, leaving no chance at unraveling this mystery.

He was sure of only one thing—his enemy must be stopped!

Darby and Strobridge entered the next car and collapsed with weariness. Up on the trestle, and fully exposed to the blizzard, the coach actually rocked. It was going to be a long night.

Wesley Bryant huddled beneath the trestle, cursing and trying to think of a way that he could finish this job and escape undetected. He and two others crouched in the last car that had crashed into the gorge. The car was on its side, a twisted, mangled ruin. Windowless, it was like a squashed can and Bryant and his men had worked hard to clear working space by shoving aside busted crates of tools, hardware and tins of peaches and beans.

Now they were watching him, expecting his orders. "I want to complete this job so the trestle and every car on it is completely destroyed."

One of the men shivered. "But, Mister Bryant, we did what we came to do."

"Not entirely. I know Strobridge. He'll have this gorge respanned in a week. No! It's not good enough, I say!"

"Then what choice do we have?" the second man pleaded. "We can't stay down here and freeze to death. And even if we lasted the night, they'd find us in the morning and start asking questions about all these explosives."

"That's right, sir," the other somberly agreed. "The way I figure, the only thing left to do is tote this dynamite up the hill a ways, bury it and rejoin the others. That way. . . ."

"Shut up!" Bryant gritted. He jammed a finger upward. "At this very minute, I've got Buckingham *and* Strobridge directly overhead. They're just sitting up there, waiting this blizzard out and trying to decide their next move."

His breath came in clouds of vapor. A candle flickered inside the wrecked car while the wind screeched outside.

"There has got to be a way to drop them and this entire trestle for keeps."

"There isn't, I tell you! I'm the explosives expert here and there's no way to light those fuses in this storm and expect the charges to detonate."

Bryant glanced up. "What about tomorrow? This thing might blow over by morning."

"So it does? Who's going to be the one to light the charges, knowing it's impossible to get out alive; either they'd shoot you from up above or, for certain, the thing would explode before we could escape." His voice dropped. "Listen, Mister Bryant, we did what you paid us for. If this storm keeps up a few days, they'll never fix that trestle. Like you said, the tunnel camps above will get starved out. But we got to get out of here! They know we came down with you."

"Dammit, there has to be a way! I'll never get Buckingham and Strobridge together again like this!"

Bryant rubbed his long fingers back and forth across his temples, willing an answer. A hundred possibilities flashed through his nimble brain and he rejected them in milliseconds. Then, in his deepest levels of concentration, the answer snaked out of the depths of his mind; it jolted him as though he'd been shocked by lightning and he whispered, "Yes! That's it."

"What?"

Bryant opened his eyes as though emerging from a satisfying dream. "We'll tie sticks of explosive to the foundation. Big bundles as high as we can reach. Then, tomorrow, or as soon as visibility improves enough for everyone to work, one of you will pot-shot the dynamite sticks. It'll all come down at once."

"Now . . . now, wait just a minute, Mister . . . ."

Bryant grabbed him by the shirtfront. "Are you telling me it won't work?"

"Yes, but . . ."

He relaxed, let go of the man and smiled. When he spoke, his voice was at once completely reasonable and reassuring. "Relax. I understand your concern. But, listen, whoever does it will be all the way across the gorge and hidden in the pines. No one will see him and, when his first bullet hits the sticks of explosive, no one on that trestle could possibly survive. I'm talking about the easiest shot of your life and by far the most profitable."

"How profitable?"

Bryant smiled. "Oh, how about a thousand now, another thousand later? That's enough to last a long time."

They agreed enthusiastically as he knew they would. They even began to argue as to who would do the job. And, just to avoid conflict and to make doubly sure there were no problems, Bryant let them both accept his offer. They inspected their rifles, then he sent them off to scout out their positions while he cheerfully began to wrap the bundles of explosives. Despite his discomfort from the cold, he began to whistle with sharp expectancy for the greatest, most spectacular fireworks display ever seen by mankind. He'd have a ringside seat, too, up in the pines, where they'd be certain to see his signal. Yes, and he'd be the only man standing on solid ground. The one and only.

It was daybreak and the blizzard had spent its fury when Darby opened his eyes to see Wesley Bryant shoulder his way inside and brush off a thick covering of snow.

The man looked positively frozen but still managed to smile at them. "They told me you two were holed up in the car nearest to the damage. You going to sleep all day, or get to work?"

"Stow it," Darby growled, pushing a couple of bags of chilled potatoes aside and standing to yawn. What he wouldn't give for a pot of scalding coffee!

Strobridge came right to the point. "You've been down in the gorge. What's it like?"

"It's cold as the grave and about as inviting," Bryant answered, his expression turning serious. "Everyone who rode the train over is dead. I'd estimate that at least a hundred feet of trestle were destroyed. Wouldn't have been half that except the locomotive knocked out the rest."

"Any sign of who did it?" Darby asked eagerly.

"Surely you joke, Mister Buckingham. It's been snowing hard enough to obliterate any tracks which might have been there."

"Blast!"

"Yes, it was a blast. Ripped out sixty feet of pilings and the locomotive took the remainder. The whole thing looks like a pile of kindling. You've quite a job cut out for you, Harvey."

"If we can build 'em, we can sure as hell fix them," the superintendent snapped irritably as he flung the door open. "Good! The weather is clearing. I'll get the Chinese to work. First thing we have to do is to pull that lead car back onto the trestle. Afterward, we'll get all of 'em to solid ground."

Darby blinked. "By hand?"

"Yep. The only other thing to do would be for someone to climb up the nearest telegraph pole and wire for another locomotive. But I forgot to bring a telegrapher and I don't aim to wait while someone goes after one. Then, too, the locomotive that did its nosedive was equipped with Crocker's new snowplow. It was the only plow I know of on the west coast that has a chance at getting this high up the Sierras."

Darby sighed. "Then what are we here for? If no other train can get through. . . ."

Strobridge grinned cynically. "Friend Buckingham, until we get this trestle fixed, there's no sense in worrying about our next move. Agreed?"

He nodded with resignation. The man was right. There came a point in the struggle when you didn't dare look anymore at the entire string of endless difficulties, but just had to face them one by one. But blast it anyway! First, they must pull what remained of the train to safety, then fix the trestle, then worry about a new locomotive and how it could break through the drifts, then. . . .

Darby ground his teeth with frustration and followed Strobridge outside into a bright, crystalline morning. What the heck, he thought, he'd never experienced pulling a dangling train car up from the brink of extinction—a test which undoubtedly would test their ingenuity.

And his nerve, too, as it became increasingly evident to the western dime novelist. They'd started by roping and chaining the front three cars in place so that they wouldn't be dragged into the gorge when the others were uncoupled. Then, one by one, they'd pushed the cars back off the trestle until only the first three remained.

"What now?" Darby asked, balancing on the slippery crossties and waiting to see what Strobridge planned next.

The man walked clear to the end of the track and his

face was thoughtful as he surveyed the first car, noting how it tilted on the edge. Finally, he shook his head regretfully and inspected the coupling.

"We can't pull it up," he grudgingly conceded. "Once we cut it loose from these other two, it would drag an army over the edge."

"So let it go!" Darby swore. "One train car more or less isn't worth risking everyone's life."

"True, I'd be inclined to agree, except for one thing."

"What's that?"

"Like some of the others, it's probably loaded with explosives."

Darby's mouth fell open. He didn't have to be told what would happen if it went over and exploded at the base of the trestle.

"Are you sure?"

"Nope. But there's only one way to find out," the man said fatalistically.

"Surely . . ." Darby swallowed drily and, though the temperature was below freezing, he felt sweat beading across his chest and face. "Surely you aren't proposing to climb up inside that thing!"

"Well, I was hoping you'd do it for me," Strobridge said, half in jest but half serious.

"You must be crazy!"

"Yeah. Guess so." He started to climb up.

"Wait a minute," Darby ordered. "You can't go in there. If anything goes wrong, you'll be needed out here."

"True." Strobridge grinned for the first time in weeks. "Well, Buckingham, you wanted a story. Get in there and find it."

Darby sighed. "Yes, I wanted a story, all right, but I also wanted to live to write it."

"Don't worry. The car is chained and roped. I'll grab a rifle and stand guard. But if I yell, you come running; 'cause it means this baby is about to go and I'll be pulling the coupling pin. Understand?"

"Of course," Darby said, clambering onto the tilted platform. If there were explosives inside, they'd be at the far end—in the car dangling in the air. Wonderful!

"Good luck, Derby Man!"

"Thanks. Just don't pull that pin before I get out," he said. "It would be a rough ride."

"Not really. The ride itself would be glassy smooth. It's the landing you'd find uncomfortable."

Darby laughed as he cast a peek down into the gorge. If he went over with the coach, he'd never live to feel a thing—especially if there were explosives inside.

Wesley Bryant knew it was time. Strobridge, one hand on the coupling pin and the other motioning frantically, had waved the coolies off the trestle. That was fine. Bryant didn't care if they lived or died, they just didn't count.

So it was just the two men alone on the trestle now. A shame old Charles Crocker himself hadn't joined this party, but no sense in turning down an opportunity. Bryant stepped behind the others, removed his hat and waved for the shooting to commence.

He saw the riflemen dark against the trees, halfway up the opposite side of the gorge.

They could not miss!

But they did. They missed because they weren't marksmen and didn't understand that firing downhill over glaring ice and snow with numb and trembling hands was an expert's game. They each expended three rounds and cursed because their slugs did not mark their impact as they might have against dirt or rock.

Darby Buckingham was halfway along the length of the coach when the first pair of rifle shots rang across the gorge. He froze, hanging onto a wall brace, then scrambled back up the inclined floor as fast as he could move.

Strobridge opened fire and hollered, "Get out of there, Buckingham!"

He was trying. How he was trying! But the car shifted downward and it pitched him to the floor and rolled him all the way down the aisle to smash against dozens of cases of explosives.

"Get out!" Strobridge bellowed again, this time with panic driving his words.

"I'm trying!"

Suddenly, the floor seemed to fall away as a great eruption punched the car sideways.

This is it! he thought. The end.

But a jerk brought the falling sensation to an abrupt halt as the coach twisted; then metal screeched as trestle timbers punctured the walls, ripping it like lead shot through a bean can. In one final moment, Darby saw the opening and lunged. He scrambled through the hole, realizing the car was impaled on the trestle and slowly was ripping open.

Fear-driven, he launched forward to attack the only way out, up through the timberworks.

Near the top Strobridge tried to reach down but couldn't, so he jammed the hot barrel of his rifle through the tracks and Darby took it and hauled himself up the last six feet to the rails.

As Darby jumped erect, he caught a glimpse of two snowy figures shooting with grim desperation at the trestle footings. No one had to tell him what they were doing—he understood and, even more, he alone knew for certain that the impaled coach was loaded with explosives.

"Let's get out of here!"

"No. I can't," Strobridge cried. "They've planted dynamite on the footings. Two more left. If they. . . ."

Darby would have liked to explain that when the coach plunged, the entire gorge would be wiped clean, trestle, three coupled cars and everything! Yes, he'd have explained it all except there was no time. So, instead, while Strobridge was reloading his rifle, Darby just punched him. Right behind the ear in a way he'd learned during his prize-fighting years. The blow knocked the superintendent unconscious and Darby snatched him up and threw him across his shoulders.

Then he began to run, as well as a man could run on an icy plank suspended eighty feet in the air.

Behind him, he heard a tortured sound as the coach began to shred. Ropes snapped with brittle pops as the anchored cars jolted forward.

Chains went next. They burst and slammed like rockets against the cars as everything jerked toward the chasm.

Then he was beyond it, striving for solid ground while, behind him, a great thundering reverberation split the mountain air and the three cars shot off the trestle. For an instant nothing happened, and then the entire gorge erupted, rolled and buckled as the explosive burst through steel and riddled every living thing for four hundred yards in any direction. Trees and the trestle splintered asunder as though the very particles of wood and fiber sought disunion.

And two men on the far slope simply ceased to exist.

Chapter 12

Wesley Bryant had been the first man to help Darby Buckingham after he'd leapt off the trestle and, now that the shock and destruction had temporarily paralyzed the survivors, he was the first to speak.

"It's the worst disaster I can imagine," he intoned. "There's no way that Harvey can get that trestle rebuilt before spring. And Crocker's snowplow is totally destroyed."

Darby pivoted and gazed at what remained of the locomotive and cars. Twisted hunks of mangled metal, and the great trestle itself blown to smithereens.

"We'll have to set up a human chain to carry provisions on up to the tunnels," he said quietly.

"You could do that," Bryant conceded, "but to what advantage? The snow drifts are too deep for other trains to get even this far, and by bringing our workers down here, we mire them in grueling and unproductive work."

"It's not unproductive," Darby said stubbornly. "As long as we can keep chipping away in those tunnels, we're making progress."

Bryant scowled. "Yes, but at what cost? Maybe you don't realize this, but our company is nearly bankrupt. Wouldn't it be better if we simply dismissed the crews until spring? The financial savings would be enormous!"

"Perhaps," Darby mused, "but it seems to me you're forgetting something very important."

"What's that?"

"We're in a race. And you don't stop to regroup if you intend to win."

"True enough. But you must also realize that there's more at stake than Mister Crocker and friends earning a fortune in land and revenues subsidized by Congress—lives

103

must be considered. How many more of Crocker's pets are
you willing to lose in order to win this fine race?"

"I . . . I don't know," Darby said in a hushed voice. "But
we can't quit now. Seems to me we've started something here
that is bigger than just profits and losses. This country
needs . . . desperately needs, a transcontinental railroad. It
would reap enormous benefits for everyone."

"Like hell it would!" Bryant spat. "What it will do is
make a handful of railroad barons rich at the expense of
small business. I'm telling you that's wrong as hell!"

Bryant's face was bitter. Twisted and hateful. Darby was
astounded at the venomous reaction, considering it came
from the Central Pacific's chief purchasing agent.

"I don't know what you're talking about."

"I'm talking about the existing freight companies who've
kept supplies flowing for years between California and Nevada. And about a hundred other businesses ranging from
Panama steamship companies to Alaskan timber and ice
concerns."

Darby glanced up sharply. "If you feel that way, why are
you on the railroad's payroll?"

Bryant opened his mouth to say something, then seemed
to reconsider. "Maybe . . . maybe I just like trains," he said
lamely. "Then again, I've got to eat like everyone else."

"Nonsense!" Darby growled. "You're the kind of man
who could succeed anywhere. Why don't you tell me what's
really on your mind?"

Wesley Bryant drew a smile with his lips. "This," he
said, making an elegant sweeping gesture with his out
stretched hand. "This destruction of lives and property."

"Sabotage. One way or another, I'll find out who's
behind this."

"Haven't we already? I mean, we all saw the culprits die
in the gorge."

"Hirelings, no doubt," Darby grumbled. "And whoever
hired them is still at large and has no intention of quitting."

"I hope you're wrong," Bryant said thoughtfully, "because, as yet, we haven't a clue as to their motive or
identity."

"You've just given me the motive," Darby said. "I hadn't
realized, though I should have, that so many small businesses
stand to fail if this railroad is completed. They've got to be
behind this."

"Oh, I doubt it," Bryant replied. "Even the most bitter among them would agree that you can't stand in the way of progress."

"Maybe not," Darby answered, "but I'd still like to talk more with you concerning specific businesses which stand to gain if the transcontinental railroad fails."

"Sure," Bryant quipped. "Anytime. But I think you're on the wrong track."

"No pun intended, I'm sure. But you just might have the key to what's behind all of these attacks."

Bryant's eyebrows lifted in mock amazement, yet there was steel underlying the banter in his voice. "Well now, wouldn't that be something."

Darby nodded. He was beginning to wonder. Was it preposterous to suspect this man who, only a few days earlier, had saved Crocker's life? It was an intriguing question indeed.

Strobridge was livid when he regained his senses; yet, if ever entered his mind to retaliate for Darby's punch, he never let on because he had too many other things to accomplish. He began by ordering Chen Yun to send crews of his people down into the gorge to clear debris and set new footings. Other men were dispatched to chop down trees and section lumber, while a third party unloaded the railroad cars and rigged up canvas packs in which to haul food and supplies up to the tunnels.

They worked halfway through the night while the temperatures plunged to nearly zero and the stars hung frigidly in an indigo sky. But the next morning, there was hot food and coffee, and tea and rice for the Chinese.

"I've pulled away almost a thousand men from my tunnels," Strobridge grumbled, "and that's a price."

"One you had to pay," Darby said, clapping his hands together and wondering if he'd ever get warm again. "You've unloaded the cars and the timber is almost ready for footings. What's left?"

"Clearing track to this point. What good is all this if the train can't break through?"

"None."

"That's right. I'm heading down the line to study the low levels. Want to come?"

Darby nodded.

"Good. Bring your pad and pencil. I'd like you to tak
notes. We'll travel on snowshoes. Do you think you can keep
up?"

"Certainly!"

Strobridge almost smiled. "You'll catch on quic
enough."

Darby spent the rest of the afternoon "catching on" t
the darned things. They were big and awkward and his shor
powerful legs weren't helping either. Still, he did his best an
was grateful that it was all downhill. They made eight mile
before darkness fell and they took shelter in an abandone
Central Pacific line shack. A roaring fire and a bottle c
brandy restored their life spirits even as their wet clothe
steamed dry.

"Drifts are over ten feet in places," Strobridge said.

"But they average less than two or three," Darby com
mented, puffing contentedly on his cigar.

"That's true. A locomotive will cut it easy except for th
drifts. In the morning we'll get one of our engines at Colfa
But there isn't a one built that can go through drifts lik
we've seen. And as fast as the Chinese could dig 'em ou
they'd fill again with wind-driven snow." He shook his hea
and pulled on the bottle. "Digging them clear just isn't th
long-term solution."

"What else can you do?"

Strobridge lay back and closed his eyes. "Would yo
mind taking a memo?"

"I suppose not. To whom?"

There was a long pause. "Make it to the Railroa
Commission, United States Congress."

Darby grabbed his paper and pencil as Harvey Stro
bridge began to dictate, choosing his words with great care.

*As Chief of Construction for the Central Pa-
cific Railroad, I have decided that a series of snow
tunnels must be constructed over a distance of some
forty miles between Cape Horn and Donner Pass.*

The pencil in Darby's hand jerked to a stop. "Fort
miles! Why that would be a colossal effort!"

Strobridge didn't even blink. He seemed mesmerized b
the fire. "Of course, it will. That's why I'm writing th
directly to Congress. Maybe I should go through Crocke

Huntington, Hopkins and Stanford. But I'm bypassing them in hope that Congress might accept this news as more creditable from an engineering viewpoint."

"I understand."

"Good. You can change my wording whichever way you want so that it sounds better. In fact, I'm counting on your help." He sighed. "Let's see. All right, here we go again.

> While this work must begin now on a few vital sections, their combined distances are not more than seven to ten miles and I am proceeding with them immediately. In my professional opinion, two types of construction should be adopted—sheds for deep cuts where the drifts accumulate, and one-sided galleries built into the mountainside with roofs sloping at angles conforming to the mountain. In this way, the avalanches will slide over the roof and down into the valley below. This is necessary because no timbering method exists to support an avalanche. The sheds and galleries will not be continuous but in sections wherever needed. They must be soundly constructed and able to withstand enormous pressures, both vertical and lateral. Their foundations will be concreted into stone and their timbers of highest quality, utilizing interlocking crossbeams. I estimate that it will require over sixty million board feet plus a thousand tons of bolts, spikes and other hardware. The cost of construction will be two million dollars."

This time the pencil actually skipped out of Darby's hand. "Two million!"

"At least. And that isn't counting maintenance or the chance that they might all burn down next summer in a forest fire."

Darby swallowed. "I think we'd better not mention that."

"Fine with me." Strobridge pulled the blankets up around his neck and closed his eyes.

"Derby Man?"

"What?"

"You write it up good. Tell Congress that without the money to build those snowsheds, there isn't a snowplow

made nor enough locomotives in this country to push through
these Sierras. Up near Donner Pass, there are places where
the drifts get forty feet deep. Tell them bureaucrats that their
mighty transcontinental railroad is going to be an impossibili-
ty except in fair weather."

Darby nodded. "It's hard to believe that tons of steam
and steel can be vanquished by nothing greater than a
snowflake."

"Not *a* snowflake. More like a billion or so of them,"
Strobridge replied.

Darby was too content and exhausted to argue and so he
asked, "Do you think we'll get the two million?"

"Probably not," Strobridge yawned. "Crocker says Congress isn't too happy with us now. They're giving their favors
to our rival 'cause she's rolling across Nebraska as fine as you
please."

Darby thought about that long after his companion
began to snore. Far into the night, he fed the stove and
polished the memo with great care because he'd never written
to the United States Congress before. He had no doubt
whatsoever that the snowsheds and galleries were vital to the
Central Pacific. Maybe it was time that Congress realized
exactly what was going on here—including sabotage. With
that in mind, Darby added a footnote and signed his name.

It was after midnight when he finished and the footnote
had become an entire page. He detailed, with what he hoped
would be viewed as unbiased reporting, how the railroad had
withstood savage treachery.

Then, he pitched the stump of his cigar into the little
cast iron stove and went to bed. Though he was bone weary
it took him a long, long time to go to sleep. He was thinking
about Wesley Bryant and how, right at this very moment, he
was in temporary charge of rebuilding the Butte Canyon
trestle.

They reached the telegraph and relay office at Colfax the
next afternoon. There was no locomotive available and Strobridge was furious. "Wire Sacramento!" he roared. "Tell
them to attach whatever kind of snowplow they've got and
hook up every locomotive in their yards. We're going to bust
on through or die trying."

"Yes, sir! But they don't have a snowplow that will . . . ."

"Don't tell me about what they *don't* have! All I car

bout is what they *do* have. Dammit, man, tell them to weld a
iece of flattened boiler-plate over the cow catcher if neces-
ary. But get 'em up here!"

The man sprinted to his telegraph and began pounding
ut the message over the fifty-four-mile distance.

Strobridge whirled on the others. "All right, you bunch
f pencil and paper pushers, grab axes and coats and get on
p the line."

"What for?" a bewildered man asked.

"For wood! We aren't waiting for anyone. Hell, by the
me those locomotives get here, I want us to have a dozen
ords stacked and ready. Steam, man! That's our power. And
: takes lots of wood. So, move!"

They bolted for the door and Darby followed. He'd
arned how to handle an axe with the best of men since
ining the Central Pacific. And he liked the feel it gave to his
rm muscles.

"Hold up, Darby. I need you here because I've decided
e can't wait to send your letter. We'll telegraph it directly to
Vashington, D.C."

"You can do that without me," Darby protested.

"Sure I can. Just thought their answer might be another
age in history. Stick around and be a part of it."

He didn't argue. Days of hard slogging through snow
1d his near fatal experience on the trestle had worn him
own. Even his pants seemed baggy. A worrisome thing. For
aame, if a Buckingham's weight ever faded below two-thirty.
arby glanced around. Surely these men would have a good
pply of food, maybe even one of those mouth-watering
ams he so dearly loved. But first, he carefully wrote a
orter version of the previous night's letter and gave it to the
legrapher. The man, smallish and bespectacled, read it
iickly. Then he read it again.

"C'mon!" Strobridge groused. "What's the matter?"

"Sir . . . sir, beggin' your pardon, but I don't think you'd
:tter send this—not after this telegram I passed through
:sterday."

The bluster went out of the superintendent's voice as he
hispered, "let me see it."

He read the message and his expression grew bleak and
intry. Then he silently dropped it on the floor and walked
utside into the snow.

Darby retrieved the telegram. It was from C. P. Hunt-

ington in Washington and several key sentences blazed up,
caught his eye and then deadened his heart.

> *Because of the recent years of Civil War,*
> *Congress unable to grant additional funds. Public*
> *attitude based on eastern newspapers skeptical of*
> *our progress. We* must *accomplish something dra-*
> *matic or we are finished.*

This time, it was Darby who let the message slip between
his fingers. Something dramatic. How about simple survival?
That, in itself, had been dramatic.

Darby patted the telegrapher on the shoulder. "You
were right," he said softly. "File that for another day."

Then, he went out to see Strobridge. Maybe, together
they could come up with something. All they needed was one
of those ordinary, everyday miracles.

Chapter 13

They arrived at Butte Canyon four days later, with Darby and Strobridge perched high up on top of the makeshift snowplow and three locomotives breathing fire and smoke. Yes, it had been tremendously difficult to bust and buck their way up the line from Colfax; but they'd made it because they had to. And, even more important, right behind was another train coming up the mountain pulling cars stocked with fresh provisions, supplies and enough explosives to replace that which had annihilated the Butte Canyon trestle and the ill-fated ambushers.

"Would you look at that!" Strobridge exclaimed. "Wes Bryant has really been driving our Chinese."

Darby was as amazed as anyone at the progress Chen Yun and his men had made in so short a time. All the big timber footings were planted and the upper sections crossbeamed. Furthermore, even though he wasn't an engineer, Darby had seen enough trestles to know that this one was properly constructed.

"It's a hell of a good job!" Strobridge breathed with admiration. "Wes Bryant said he could read blueprints and had some construction background, but I never expected him to be half this far along. I'd have been pleased if he'd just dug and set the footings in mortar."

"Apparently, our Mister Bryant is a man of great and varied talents," Darby mused thoughtfully. "I wonder what else he's capable of."

"Huh?"

"Never mind. Just thinking aloud."

Strobridge's look was curious. "Best watch yourself, Derby Man. That's the first sign of old age."

Before the writer could phrase a suitable answer, Strobridge was on his way to congratulate Bryant.

"Damnation, Wes!" he bellowed heartily. "You've really been moving things. I'm going to ask Crocker to transfer you to construction. You're too damn good to waste on ledgers and cost figures. How about it?"

The man laughed. "Well, I have enjoyed the challenge. Facing this mountain stirs up the blood."

"Sure it does! Damned if I haven't misjudged you!"

"Do you think Crocker would allow me to switch from administration?"

"Hell, yes! We're up against it now. You and me and Darby are all going to have to come up with a miracle in the next few days. Ain't that right?"

Darby nodded and his eyes probed Bryant. The man avoided his gaze and, after a minute, Darby strode away to inspect the trestle. It just didn't seem possible that Bryant could have gotten so much done since they'd last been here. But yet, here it stood—absolutely textbook in its perfection.

"What the devil took you so long!" Crocker thundered when they arrived. "My God, do you expect me to oversee the construction of eight tunnels? Not that it matters after the telegram I received a few days ago. We're dead."

Darby's expression was grim. "I take it you are aware of the bad news."

"Aware of it? Sure. But I refuse to knuckle under and give up because of a bunch of woolly brained politicians."

"What about the money?" Bryant asked. "Sir, this railroad now has over twelve thousand men on its payroll. Our expenses exceed twenty-five thousand dollars a day."

"Hang the expenses!"

Bryant curbed his reply—when Crocker got his back up, he was impossible to reason with. Everyone knew that. He turned to Darby and Strobridge. "You two had better explain what we've been talking about."

"Talking about?" The big railroad president's eyes danced. "Got a plan, do you? Something dramatic?"

The western dime novelist was one of the few men whose sheer physical presence could overshadow Crocker. "Yes, we think so."

"Good! Let's go to my office and hear about it. Whatever

you three may have in mind has got to be better than giving up."

Ten minutes later, when the whiskey had been poured and cigars lit all around, Crocker nodded impatiently. His face reflected controlled excitement. "Let's hear it, Derby Man."

"All right. To begin with, we all know that capturing the fancy and purse strings of Congress is no easy task. They understand nothing of the engineering problems we face in blasting these tunnels. Really, all they care about is progress."

"Go on," Crocker said, nodding vigorously. "Get straight to the point."

"Very well. Harvey and I agree we should bypass the tunnels."

"What!" Crocker boomed.

"Bypass them, I said. We both feel that the only hope left is to put an entire railroad on our backs and haul it over Donner Pass—clear into Nevada."

Crocker rocked back in his chair. "Is it possible?"

"Of course not!" Bryant railed. "I've been trying to argue some sense into these two for days."

"You're wrong," Strobridge spat, "though I admit there's a good chance we'll fail and lose both men and equipment. In fact, I think it only candid to admit the odds are against us." His eyes raked their faces. "But, dare we not try?"

Crocker looked away. He rose to his feet and paced in silence before answering. "Harvey, you're our Chief of Construction. There's not a man alive who could possibly succeed other than yourself. Are you . . . are you sure you want us to make the attempt?"

"Certainly. If we don't, I'm out of a job, because the Central Pacific Railroad is finished."

"Buckingham?"

He smiled and his black mustache bristled with anticipation. "I've talked to Chen Yun and he says his people are ready. As for me, I've got a book to write when this is all over and I want it to end in triumph a long way to the east when we hook up with the Union Pacific. I say yes."

Crocker turned to the sole dissenter. "You seem to be outnumbered."

"Yeah. Well," Bryant said cryptically, "so it would appear. But they're still dead wrong. The plan is madness. I know, because I'm the one who buys our engines and rolling stock."

"What the hell has that got to do with anything?" Strobridge demanded.

Bryant flushed with anger and took a deep breath. "Do any of you people realize that our standard locomotive, which generates from 110 to 125 pounds of steam pressure, has an empty weight of between sixty-two and seventy-five *thousand* pounds? We are talking about moving roughly thirty-five tons of machinery!"

They lapsed into silence, except for Darby who cleared his throat and said, "I'm no engineer and won't even attempt to counter what we've just heard. All I know is this—people can do almost anything they believe in."

Bryant started to interrupt but Darby cut him off short. "Hear me out. I've seen runts and weaklings whip physically superior men just because they had the grit to make it possible. And we've all witnessed how the Chinese ripped a roadbed across the face of Cape Horn. Everyone thought that was impossible. Now, our opposition would have us believe we can't beat Donner Pass. We've listened to uninformed politicians and read every ignorant critic who's taken a crack at writing a newspaper column. Are we really so callow as to listen to those whose greatest hope is that we fail?"

No one looked at him. Their eyes were downcast. Darby was angry and he plunged on. "I'm a pretty decent historian and I recall there was once a man named Hannibal who faced something every bit as formidable as these Sierras. Same conditions—winter, snow and mountains so big and rugged they'd shadow a hundred miles. But he went ahead and attacked them anyway. And I'll bet you if he'd listened to the craven voices of pessimism, he'd never even have tried. Why, I'm sure his head elephant drivers all said crossing the Alps was impossible, and told him that those huge beasts would sink and die."

He gazed unwaveringly at Crocker. "You know the decision Hannibal made. Not an easy one. Probably as desperate as this one you face. But he made it because *he had no choice*. I submit, Mister Crocker, this situation is identical. Be as Hannibal—know we can do it because we must. Let us make history!"

For almost a full minute no one said another word. Then

Crocker took a deep breath. He stood up and seemed to grow taller. "Gentlemen, I wasn't going to say this, but while you were down at Butte Canyon, I discovered a spy in our midst. He was an engineer for the Union Pacific Railroad. He spent all his time studying and measuring each of our tunnels."

"Where is he?" Strobridge roared. "I'll kill him with my bare hands!"

"I anticipated that reaction and let him go after scaring him out of his wits," replied Crocker. "But, before I did, he told me that his conclusion was that it would take us *three years* to blast the Summit Tunnel under Donner Pass."

"That's preposterous!"

"Of course it is, but I believe we cannot prevent that conclusion from reaching Washington and Congress. That's why I agree we must temporarily bypass the tunnels."

Crocker's voice lifted dramatically. "Think of the sensation it will cause. First the spy's report of three years, then our own thundering announcement that we *will* be in Nevada within three months."

He slapped his chubby hands together. "Gentlemen, such a feat would capture the nation's heart. That's why I'm prepared to accept all responsibility for this endeavor. Tonight, I will telegraph my three partners and receive their support and, tomorrow, the assault begins. God willing, we will prevail as did Hannibal in the Alps!"

My dear Miss Beavers:

It is late and, outside, we are experiencing yet another blizzard which has brought the snow level here at Donner Pass to a depth of over twenty feet. I am still trying to unravel the mystery of who is behind the sabotage. It is my suspicion that the culprit is none other than Mister Crocker's young nephew, the fellow you met during our last evening together, Philip Rait.

He has fallen completely out of favor here and has become rather unkempt and wild-eyed. I intend to watch him every moment. Another suspect is a man named Wesley Bryant. However, my suspicions are waning in his case, as he has worked tirelessly and rather heroically since becoming directly involved in railroad construction.

These past few months, we have taken three thousand Chinese over Donner Summit to grade and bridge the eastern slope of these Sierras all the way past Donner Lake, clear beyond Truckee to the Nevada line. Now there is nothing to do but perform the miracle of hauling three locomotives and forty railroad cars over the pass. We are all confident it can be done. Tomorrow, weather and God permitting, we shall see. Until then, my sweet, wish us well.

Sincerely,
Darby Buckingham

"Are we ready?" Darby asked.

"As much as we'll ever be," Strobridge replied tightly.

Darby stared at the two stripped down locomotives, even with their smokestacks and huge drive wheels missing, they were awesome, sitting crouched on their specially constructed sleds. They were huge, hulking black beetle-like objects chained as though they might suddenly come to life and destroy their captors.

Sixty oxen and five hundred Chinamen were going to pull these monsters up over the nearby summit, then keep them from plunging down the eastern slopes into Donner Lake.

"Let's go!" Strobridge cried at the top of his voice.

Though it wasn't necessary, Chen Yun echoed the order in Chinese. They knew what had to be done and that, assuming they survived this journey, two more locomotives awaited, along with freight cars and enough iron rails to cover fifty miles of the previously graded eastern slope.

At the cry, beasts and men threw themselves against their ropes and chains and harness. For one agonizing moment, nothing happened. Then, realizing his foolishness, Darby plowed through the snow, grabbed a link of chain and leaned into the pull. His muscles bunched, his head seemed to sink into his massive shoulders and a great cry split the air as it was wrenched from his lungs.

"Ahhhh!"

And, miraculously, the sleds budged. An inch, then a foot, then they were plowing forward over the packed snow and crunching up the trail.

The push for the Donner Pass Summit continued for nearly a week. Fortunately the weather held, although it was bitterly cold and the Chinese dropped from sheer exhaustion. But they made it. And, in the moment when they conquered the Summit and gazed out to the vast panorama of desert only thirty miles eastward, every man among them felt an overpowering sense of triumph and awe at their own accomplishment.

Behind them lay a path of snowy heartache and, before them . . . well, before them stretched the gateway to Nevada—the starting point of a race they'd given everything just to enter. Though the sun was driving downward, they spurned rest and begged to use the last hours of that glorious day to push on toward the distant warmth and sunlight.

Crocker let them, knowing he must. And so they edged forward, rigging chains to the trees so that the engines might not break free and slide out of control toward the ice-blue waters of Donner Lake.

"Why not finish?" Darby urged. "Just another half-mile and we're on flat ground."

Strobridge looked worried. "I don't know. This final stretch along the side of the hill is damn steep."

"Yes, but look at all the trees on the upper side we can chain up to. Besides, you know that none of us could sleep tonight with the locomotives resting on this grade. And if it snows, we'd be in serious trouble by morning."

Strobridge estimated the distance to the bottom, noted how the last hundred yards were barren of anchoring trees.

"It'll be dark in an hour. Can we finish?"

"I think we'd better try," Darby said resolutely. The thought of leaving the engines so near to the bottom seemed pointless. Besides, he figured tonight they'd bed down in one of the Central Pacific's makeshift cabins by the lake and celebrate their achievement. He'd been cold and sleeping on ice for too long. To be dry and warm had become an even greater obsession than food.

"Let's go then," Strobridge said tightly. "We'll double up and take them down one at a time."

The Chinese and the oxen were experienced and there was little need for Chen Yun to interpret directions as they lined out down the slope with the first huge locomotive. Chain and rope spun outward to wrap around trees and be held. The boat-like sleds protested under the weight of thirty-five tons, then began to slide downhill—downhill toward the ice-covered Donner Lake.

It went well. Snow-covered trees quivered bravely as the great chains were wound and unwound. And there was no sideways slippage.

Then they passed the anchoring trees onto the lowest section of the mountainside where the snow was glassy with ice, and everyone's heart pounded faster. Another hundred yards. No more, just . . .

Rifle shots whacked into them from above. They were exposed and unprotected; two Chinese screamed and collapsed, staining the snow crimson as they died. A third was knocked over and began to wail as he flopped around beneath the locomotive. Everyone was shouting and the bullets kept spinning them around, scattering them as they ran.

Darby shouted for the Chinese to drop and lie still, but no one heard him over the booming rifle and shrill, chattering voices. And then the huge locomotive began to slide off the sled as men bucked through snow in terror.

It seemed to take a long, long time before the massive engine leaned out and crashed over with enough force to send shivers up the mountainside. It took even longer for those tremors to pass up the slope and loosen the deep, deep snowpack. But, in moments, with a soft whisper, the avalanche came stealing down at them, growing bigger and stronger until it was a wall of white death.

Darby saw it obliterate the upper slope and engulf the firing sniper. Then, he was running like everyone else as it all hissed down to beat against the locomotive like a tidal wave striking a New England lighthouse. The engine momentarily stole its force, stunned the avalanche and sent it showering toward the cold yellow moon. But then it passed over them, rolling and rolling until it layered across the western shores of Donner Lake.

Darby Buckingham felt himself being engulfed, smothered in coldness. He began to thrash, for he could see nothing, not even the overturned locomotive beside which he lay buried.

Chapter 14

Most survived. Either they'd been able to run out of the avalanche's path or, like Darby, they'd found themselves rolled up and under the locomotive into an air pocket. But the real saving factor was the snow itself. Powdery and dry from weeks of below-freezing temperatures, it had not packed densely.

Philip Rait III did not escape. He had been highest on the mountain. They found his body, and the rifle which had become entangled in his coat, far, far below the surface. From all indications, he'd survived the first impact and been rolled a thousand times until he'd slammed into the locomotive. Still he must have lived a while, for he had confirmed the horror frozen into his lifeless expression. He'd given it everything he had; it had been a remarkable try. But he'd failed and there wasn't a man among the crews who wasn't glad he'd died—including Wesley Bryant.

During the next few weeks, the men of the Central Pacific labored night and day to drag more rolling stock over the summit, as well as wooden ties and the quarter-ton lengths of track. Everything was reassembled at Truckee, where the elevation was still nearly six thousand feet and the temperature plunged below zero every night. No matter. They were beneath the summit and facing Nevada. And they could begin to drive rails! After the months of living and working in underground tunnels of rock and snow, to work outdoors and see the clear blue sky was a blessing.

"I'll pull most of the crews down here to lay track," Strobridge vowed. "It's not healthy to spend months underground. After the thaw, I'll send 'em back to finish their work. But for now . . . now, we're going to show the world that the Central Pacific is off and running!"

119

Darby agreed wholeheartedly. Winter and Donner Pass had taken their toll on the work crews. They were listless, vacant-eyed and thin, in spite of the best food and as much of it as they required. But now, as Strobridge and Crocker brought them down to Truckee, he noted their quickened step and the eagerness with which they began to lay track down the mountains. Bridges and trestles went up almost as if by magic as every foot of rail dropped them closer to the warm desert.

Spring was coming and never had the future looked brighter. Darby waited until the locomotives were running on their short tracks and then he wrote a telegram he hoped would force Congress to reverse its earlier funding decision.

> *Central Pacific Railroad has conquered the Sierra Nevada mountains! STOP . Greatest engineering feat in history. STOP . Tracks now being laid to Reno, Nevada. STOP . Race with Union Pacific is on. STOP . Reinstatement of funds critical. STOP . Dream of Transcontinental Railroad to become a reality. STOP .*

Crocker, Strobridge, Bryant and Darby Buckingham all watched the telegraph operator send the message. And, when it had been tapped over the lines, they waited, as though they could foresee the national reaction.

"Well," Darby said in a hushed voice, "we've given them their blasted miracle. Now, it's out of our hands."

"Huntington tells me we had to mortgage our assets just to meet this week's payroll," Crocker said quietly. "It's *got* to work or we're dead, right here in Truckee, California."

Bryant remained silent while Strobridge paced back and forth. "They'll *have* to rescind their earlier decision. What do you think, Darby?"

"We've got them," he gritted. "Within hours that telegram will flash coast-to-coast; it will be in the headlines of every newspaper in America. I expect that, by tomorrow morning, we should be receiving some pretty dramatic news —one way or the other."

He was correct. By six a.m., the telegraph was dancing as hundreds and hundreds of people tried to extend their congratulations. But only two were really needed to send the anxious Truckee participants into ecstasy. One was from C

P. Huntington and the other from President Abraham Lincoln himself. Both were laudatory. They overflowed with congratulations *and* assurances that funds would be released; indeed, an excited nation would be witnessing every mile of this epic race.

"Whoopee!" Crocker cried as they all burst out with smiles and laughter and whoops of joy.

"This calls for a celebration!" the president of the resurrected Central Pacific shouted. "Tonight, we'll quit early and every man on the payroll will have whiskey!"

"The Chinese don't drink," Darby reminded him.

"Spike their tea, man! I'll have no one holding back!"

Darby nodded. He could probably figure out some kind of a reward. But tonight . . . well, they deserved a party. And now he could see victory ahead. It was just thirty-three miles along the gushing Truckee River to Reno. Thirty-three miles, dropping 1,333 feet out of these blizzard-whipped mountains. They'd make it and soon he'd be keeping his promise to Dolly Beavers.

Dolly. The very thought of her lifted his spirits. After they got off this mountain, and when Strobridge's crews returned and finished the big Summit Tunnel over Donner Pass—well, the train would be running before this new year was past. And he'd take his good woman to San Francisco. Together, they'd revel in the finest that beautiful city had to offer.

So eager was he to spread the good news, he decided to write to her that very night.

He was not that evening's only letter writer.

Wesley Bryant excused himself from the party quite early, saying he was coming down with a chest cough and probably needed more rest.

No one had missed him. And late that night, while they celebrated, he studied reams of documents from Crocker's vault. Some, like the stock certificates of demand and various unrecorded promissory notes, he stuffed into his leather case. They would be worth several million dollars when forged with the railroad president's signature. Duplication of handwriting was another one of his special talents. He did not touch any cash, for that would be discovered with the first payroll. It might be a month before the other papers were missed.

Bryant also modified several of Theodore Judah's survey maps, in hopes that he could throw the Central Pacific off-course should his more immediate plans fail. Things, he had to admit, were quite desperate now. With the death of Philip Rait III, the last of his original conspirators was gone. Perhaps that was for the best, for he was convinced his biggest error had been in relying upon others to do what he should have done personally.

He wouldn't fail. Couldn't! The idea of defeat was completely foreign. And, after all, the Central Pacific, no matter what Darby Buckingham's telegram said, really hadn't conquered the Sierras and Donner Pass. Hell, no. They were, if the truth be known, bogged down at the Summit Tunnel. The very tunnel which a qualified Union Pacific engineer had judged three years from completion.

What earthly good was a segmented railroad—a railroad which started and ended at Summit Tunnel? A segmented. . . .

He froze. A bell seemed to clang in his brain. Then, the enormity of his discovery clicked into focus and threw him back in Crocker's desk chair. He began to laugh. And kept laughing as he took Crocker's copy of the huge and minutely detailed Railroad Act by which Congress and the Central Pacific Railroad were bound.

It took him almost forty minutes of skimming pages to find the seemingly innocuous little passage which read: *Under no circumstances whatsoever will Congress grant subsidy funds for track which is not contiguous in nature. That is, track which has not been consecutively laid without a break. The reasonability of this is self-evident and has been mutually agreed upon with. . . .*

"That's it!" he whispered, reverently squeezing the document like a lover and committing the words to memory. Wesley Bryant returned the Railroad Act to the vault and locked it before he grabbed the documents up with a swoop and headed for the door. The way of escape was clear and he exited the coach feeling very, very satisfied. And later that night, about the time the last celebrants tottered happily to bed, Bryant completed a six-page letter. He would forward a copy to a Panama steamship line along with duplicates to several local stage and freight companies that he knew would be most interested in this new and exciting discovery.

Yes, he thought, as he contentedly sealed the envelopes he'd done his part, right down to page and paragraph of the

Railroad Act—now it was their turn and they'd know exactly how to use this information because their own personal fortunes were at stake.

Mark Hopkins was almost ten years older than Charles Crocker and the other two partners who owned the Central Pacific. He was a smallish man, polite almost to the point of self-abasement, yet none of the rest could drive as shrewd a bargain. Hopkins was soft-spoken, studious and a hopeless miser. His sole passion beyond the accumulation of wealth was tending his Sacramento gardens, so that he might never run out of the peas and carrots necessary for his meager vegetarian diet. People called him Uncle Mark and, when he acted or spoke, it was always calm, deliberate and damned important.

So it was that, upon his arrival at Truckee three weeks later, he scarcely uttered a word as a surprised Charles Crocker led the neat and composed man into his office and closed the door.

An hour later, Mark Hopkins emerged alone. He acknowledged no one, but climbed stiffly into his sled for the return journey to Sacramento.

Darby thought the man's behavior extremely boorish and not a little queer. When evening came and the railroad president still hadn't emerged, Darby grew concerned enough to go to his coach and knock.

"Go away!" Crocker groaned weakly.

Darby entered. One look at the prostrate man on the sofa told him that some terrible calamity had ridden into their midst in the form of Mark Hopkins. Darby sat down beside the ghastly appearing railroad president.

"Tell me our latest misfortune from start to finish," he ordered heavily. "What has gone wrong now?"

Crocker stared up at the ceiling. When he spoke, his voice was barely audible. "They've cut our funds off entirely, Darby." In a few painful words he explained why, even directed him to the copy of the Railroad Act which lay forgotten on the carpet.

"So we're busted," Darby intoned.

"Almost. Fortunately, Huntington capitalized on your telegram and grabbed all the subsidy money that was floating around Capitol Hill. Then, with this breach of contract revelation, all monies were cut off immediately. *Nothing* will be paid until we finish those tunnels up by Donner Pass and lay track down to here."

"Can we . . . can we do it?"

"Hell no," Crocker sighed. "We could, if it weren't for the Summit Tunnel under the pass. I'm informed that all the others are pretty well done. But . . . oh hell, we're beaten . . ."

"I've heard that before around here," Darby stated. "Many times. And we've always gotten through somehow."

"Yes, but this time not even a miracle could save us," Crocker said bitterly. "Summit Tunnel can't be whipped overnight."

"How long *do* we have?"

Crocker blinked. "What do you mean? I said . . ."

Darby's voice was harsh when he interrupted. "How much money could Huntington get before the story broke? Do we have a month? Six months? What, man!"

"Mark gives us something between that. Depends on expenses. I'd guess three, perhaps four months."

"Then," Darby said, "we'd better get Harvey Strobridge and Chen Yun in here to plan strategy."

Crocker sat upright. "Don't you understand, Buckingham? They're talking about three years! I'm telling you three months!"

Darby glanced away. He was afraid that, if he stayed a minute longer, Crocker would talk him out of even trying. And that would be too bad, because the man himself would rebound by morning. It was his nature to rise up from his own emotional lows to fight back against any odds. Darby knew he was the same, only his personal black depressions were far worse and he hadn't had one for years. Not since he'd made the decision to leave New York City and come west to chronicle the frontier. No, he'd been just fine ever since and he had every intention of staying that way.

Even, he thought as he stormed out the door, if it took another miracle.

Chapter 15

Harvey Strobridge scrubbed his face wearily. Since hearing Mark Hopkins' news, he'd aged twenty years. Nevertheless, Darby knew the man was a bulldog who'd sink his fangs into a thing and hang on, until someone or something broke his neck.

Strobridge sighed after long deliberation. "Any sane construction man would advise us to pack and go home."

"Never mind that," Darby said. "What can we do?"

"Pray. That and send every Chinaman we've got up to those tunnels."

"I beg your pardon," Chen Yun said quietly, "but there is no more room to work in tunnels."

"Yeah, that's the problem, all right," Strobridge agreed. "We'd have to sink a 125-foot shaft down from the top of the pass so crews could be lowered."

"It's worth a try, isn't it?" Darby asked.

"Sure it is, but we'd still fall short. My measurements say we've gone in about six hundred feet on the west side and four-fifty on the east."

"Then we've got about six hundred more to go."

"Correct. And we can't do it in three or four months. Not even by sinking a shaft. It's that damned rock. Solid granite. If you put any more than a few ounces of black powder in each drill hole, the granite ricochets the blast into the workers' faces."

"Then maybe," Darby said evenly, "it's time we switched horses."

"What do you mean?" Crocker asked.

"I know what he means. Just figured it out," Strobridge said, looking at Darby's set expression. "Tell 'em."

125

"I mean I think we should obtain some nitroglycerin."

"No!" Crocker gasped. "I told you what happened in San Francisco."

"And I'm saying this is not San Francisco and we have no choice whatsoever."

Crocker shook his head. "Just like Hannibal."

"Exactly," Darby grunted. "Only the mountain just keeps getting taller."

"Yes, yes, it does. But you've forgotten something."

"What?"

"Nitroglycerin has been made illegal in California."

Darby lit a cigar. "Then I'll go to San Francisco, hire a chemist and import the ingredients. We'll mix it right in the tunnel. It will be nitroglycerin only as long as it takes to set up and blow. I don't think anyone will protest."

Hope flared in their eyes and it was Strobridge who blurted, "Do you really believe you can find the ingredients and a chemist who would mix them?"

Darby thought it over for about one second. "We'll tell him to name his own price. Any price, because the chips are down and it's our last draw. If I put it that way, I'll have the man and the nitroglycerin working in Summit Tunnel within ten days. Mister Crocker, it's your railroad."

"Darby, I . . . oh, hell," he grunted, slamming his fist down on his desk. "Start packing, man! You're wasting precious time!"

He made it back in nine days, with a determined little Scottish chemist by the name of James Howden who claimed to fear nothing he could mix in a flask or pound with a pestle. Besides, he assured them the ingredients were safe enough if kept apart from each other.

"Nothing to be afraid of, gentlemen," Howden said, "all we have is the glycerin itself, plus some nitric and sulphuric acids to make things happen."

"What does it look like?" Crocker asked nervously.

To this, James Howden merely shrugged and replied, "How should I know, sir? Only a lunatic or a man being paid a king's ransom would be foolish enough to mess with nitroglycerin."

Darby groaned. Strobridge and Crocker paled considerably. Later, Crocker made the comment that Howden must surely be crazy and how much did he hold out for against the Central Pacific Railroad?

"Ten thousand dollars to take us under Donner Pass."

Crocker swallowed drily. "Then he's not so crazy after all," he replied sadly as he hurried away.

Everyone waited outside the tunnel, *way* outside, until the chemist emerged, nearly twenty minutes later, with a flaskful of yellow liquid, pale colored and oily. He cradled it like a newborn baby and there wasn't a man watching who didn't retreat as far as his own personal dignity allowed when he saw the sweat of fear which bathed Howden's chalky face.

He was concentrating so intently on the bottle that he tripped over a rock. A gasp of fear sounds the same in English, Scottish, or Chinese, and more than a thousand throats echoed collectively.

"My God!" Crocker cried. *"Sit down, man!"*

Howden almost collapsed. He had the look of a man who'd seen his own headstone.

"What now?" he croaked.

"We use it," Darby said, making himself go forward as Strobridge came along. Chen Yun ordered three men to follow him into the tunnel while Howden managed to stand up and shakily trail in after.

They talked it over and, in the end, decided to drill an inch and a quarter diameter hole a foot and a half deep in the rock wall. The frightened Chinese drilled the holes, slanting downward, and Darby took the nitroglycerin and braced himself for step two. He was petrified with fear, certain that it would blow him to tiny bits the moment he poured. "Why doesn't everyone get out of here. There's no advantage in all of us being pulverized."

Chen Yun sent the workers out and Howden left with this piece of advice, "Don't spill it!"

"Well," Strobridge whispered, "let's get this over with."

"Agreed." Darby held the lip of the flask to the bore hole and tilted it up. "Please don't spill;" he prayed aloud.

It didn't. Yet, in his nervousness, a few drops overflowed and ran down the wall as they stared in horrified fascination, but nothing happened.

Next, they plugged up the hole with a wad of hay and peppered it with blasting powder. Finally, they took a fuse and fixed it lightly in place according to Howden's directions.

"That's it," Darby sighed.

"Light the damn thing and let's run. Chen Yun, are you certain the fuse is long enough?"

"Yes. We could run very far."

"Don't worry," Darby promised, "I'm planning on it!"

And run they did. Straight down the over six hundred feet of tunnel and out the western portal. Across the clearing and through the mob of onlookers who took the cue and sprinted down the mountain in a wild and frenzied retreat.

Darby finally stopped when he could run no more and common sense dictated that even nitroglycerin couldn't reach him nearly a mile away.

Gasping, dragging for air, they heard the explosion come rumbling out of the mountain, packing the force and thunder of forty locomotives and shooting granite from the tunnel's mouth like cannon shot.

"Incredible," Darby said in awe.

"Yes," Howden replied, climbing out from behind an enormous boulder, "wasn't it a bang though!"

In the days that followed, apprehension gave way to hope as the chemist mixed his daily batch of nitroglycerin. The liquid explosive was at least eight times more powerful than black powder and the tunneling rate jumped by that multiple almost from the first day. In addition to the enormous punch, nitroglycerin had other splendid advantages—it required a much smaller diameter drill hole and, after a blast, the tunnel air cleared faster than when black powder was used. Finally, the liquid worked like a charm when the rock became wet due to vertical fissures. In those cases, all that was required was to fill a small metal cartridge or even an ordinary can with black powder and fasten it over the hole with a waterproof fuse. When the black powder exploded, the highly unstable nitroglycerin followed instantly.

By the end of their first month, they finished all the western slope tunnels except the one under Donner Pass.

"Now," Strobridge vowed, "we'll see if our people still remember how to lay track."

The Chinese hadn't forgotten at all. And, because they did not have to clear snow and set the railroad ties in frozen ground in the tunnels, the rails went down fast. As soon as a lower tunnel was finished, Strobridge and Crocker moved the Chinese up to Donner Pass where the shaft was being sunk, in order that blasting might be carried on from three points.

Even so, the day finally arrived when the railroad President had to inform them that the coffers of the Central Pacific were almost empty and, in less than six weeks, they'd go broke.

"We'll make it," Darby growled, "if nothing goes wrong."

"Then we're in trouble," Crocker replied, "because something *always* goes wrong."

"Maybe. Yet, since the day when Philip Rait was buried in that avalanche while trying to ambush us, we've had no trouble."

Crocker eyed him curiously, then shook his head. "I still can't believe he actually was involved."

"Involved? Strobridge thinks he was in charge of the sabotage effort."

"Do you concur?"

"I'd like to," Darby said quietly. "Every day that passes without an accident seems to indicate that perhaps he was the head man. But. . . ."

"Hell," Crocker snorted, "you don't believe Philip was the ringleader anymore than I do. Strobridge is engaging in wishful thinking."

Yes, Darby thought as he helped to place another charge of nitroglycerin, perhaps they'd all been guilty of that because, in truth, he couldn't help but think that someone else was behind it. Just waiting for his chance. That's why he'd been trying to keep his number one candidate under surveillance whenever possible. And that was Wesley Bryant.

Wesley Bryant had a plan, yet didn't. He knew that the Central Pacific was going to win unless he stopped the tunneling under Donner Pass. There were several men who'd help him for a price he was fully prepared to pay. Besides, he reasoned, if he planned things right, they'd never survive to collect their payments.

One man, whose name he couldn't remember, was the foreman in charge of the shaft being drilled and blasted into the Summit. It had been brutal work being exposed to the raging blizzards up on top. The snowpack was thirty-eight feet deep and it had taken nearly two weeks just to reach the working surface. But the shaft wasn't going to be big, just deep enough to rig up a steam engine and hoisting cage like they were using in Virginia City. Because the shaft was much narrower than the tunnel it was attempting to reach, progress had been amazing—more than twenty feet a day until now they were over one hundred feet deep and lacked but twenty-five to reach tunnel level.

It was time to intervene.

The foreman's name, as he recalled late that night when he met him in an accommodating blizzard on Donner Summit, was Jones. William Jones listened while he outlined exactly what he wanted done and then asked, "When?"

"Right now."

"Good. The shaft is empty for the moment."

Bryant started peeling off greenbacks in denominations of one hundred. "All you have to do is simply drop a large flask of nitroglycerin into the shaft and. . . ."

"Wait a minute! Not *that* stuff."

Bryant's fist crushed the bills. "Why not?"

"Because that chemist is the only one knows how to mix it. He won't tell nobody so they can't take his job."

"Damn! Then it'll have to be dynamite. Enough to collapse the shaft."

"You're talking about a case of the stuff."

"That's right," Bryant said easily. "So let's go find one."

William Jones' eyes became veiled and crafty. "Not going to be easy. Lots of risks I'm taking."

"I understand." Bryant opened his fist, peeled off four hundred more and said, "It's cold and I'm weary of your excuses and delays. You've got a choice."

"Sure I do." The man retreated a step. "You can give me that now and as much later, or I can tell Mister Crocker about this conversation."

Bryant's eyes flashed with violence. His gunhand twitched but he willed himself to keep from reaching for it. "I see," he said with a voice that rustled like dead leaves. "It appears you've got me in a fix."

"Sure I do," Jones breathed, relief flooding his face. "I don't mean to blackmail anyone but a man's got to look out for himself. I'll never have another chance like this one."

"That's true," Bryant replied, actually smiling. "I guess you've outsmarted me."

Jones pulled his hand out of his jacket and showed the ʳstol he'd been gripping. "Jest so you know I'm not all ᵒid."

"Thank you. Truly, I've underestimated your intellect. But now, can we get on with this before we both freeze?"

Jones nodded and produced the key to the explosives shed. In minutes they had the case of dynamite and were lugging it to the shaft.

"They'd have had the steam engine installed day after tomorrow," Jones grunted. "Hoisting reel, cage and cables right after."

"Very interesting. Now show me how much fuse it will take and how to rig it up to this case."

"It might go off on impact but I don't think we'll chance it."

"Good idea," Bryant said cryptically.

"So we want it to go off before it hits bottom. That means a *very* short fuse. Like under four inches."

"I see."

Jones cut the fuse, jammed it into the box and fumbled around until he was satisfied, then clipped it in place.

"Is that all?"

"Except for lighting it."

"Then proceed."

The man hesitated. Removed his hands from his pockets and struck a match. "Well," he breathed, "I sure hate to. . . ."

He never quite finished. Bryant kicked him screaming into the pit and waited until he heard the body strike rock.

"Four seconds exactly. At least he had that much figured out right."

Then, he lit the fuse and shoved the case of dynamite into the hole. He was five strides away when all hell broke loose on Donner Pass.

Chapter 16

The explosion did not penetrate into the main tunnel under Donner Pass. Nevertheless, everyone from Charles Crocker on down to the lowest Chinaman was outraged by the heinous act of sabotage.

The shaft itself became a hundred-foot pit of rubble which would require weeks of excavation.

"We haven't time for it," Strobridge proclaimed. "I say we abandon it and concentrate on the tunnel."

"How much farther until we break through?" Crocker demanded.

"Less than a hundred feet."

"We'll go bankrupt first."

Darby stepped in between. "Before that happens, telegraph my New York bank and publisher. Perhaps my assets are sufficient to buy us a little more time."

"Thanks," Crocker said, "but I'm afraid you have no idea of the daily expenses of the Central Pacific."

"And you, sir, have no idea of my net worth." He smiled. "I should guess it sufficient to buy us a week's worth of tunneling."

"I stand in your debt," the railroad president said, emotion rich in his voice. "Let's hope your generous offer needn't be accepted. I'll order Howden to double up on the batches of nitroglycerin. He won't be happy."

"No," Darby said. "But if our chemist wants his money upon completion of the tunnel, he has no choice. I'll make that very clear to him."

"Then it's settled," Strobridge said. "Bryant, you're going to play a key part in our success or failure in the few days remaining."

The man blinked. "How?"

"You'll be in charge of the eastern entrance of Summit Tunnel. Keep your crews going nonstop on the rock face while others behind them lay rails under Donner Pass."

"Now, wait a minute! That's too dangerous."

"Coordinate!" Strobridge cried hoarsely. "Lay track in spurts between nitro blasts. That's what I'll be doing on the western side."

Wesley Bryant nodded, aware that he had absolutely no choice in the matter.

Charles Crocker stepped in. "Darby, we've saved your job for last, because it's the most important."

"Name it."

"All right, you'll be our protector. I want you anywhere and everywhere at once. You'll be responsible for protecting both Bryant and Harvey from attack."

"Are you aware of my reputation with firearms, sir?"

"Of course." Crocker actually smiled. "And also of your courage and resourcefulness. Arm yourself with a double barreled shotgun and a stick of dynamite or whatever the hell it takes to keep the saboteurs off our backs. We need *one* week! Give us that long and you've given life to the Central Pacific."

A deep, protracted silence followed that was at last broken by the writer. "You've got it," he vowed fervently. "I swear you'll have your week."

In the days which followed, Darby was a man obsessed with his pledge to protect the Summit Tunnel. Long before dawn each morning, he accompanied James Howden to his specially prepared kitchen on the western end of Donner Pass. There, like some sorcerer of old, the Scottish chemist brewed his magical elixir of destruction while Darby kept a sharp lookout for trouble.

Maybe Crocker had been joking, but the writer did begin carrying two sticks of dynamite in his coat pocket. That, plus a revolver and shotgun, made him feel like a walking bomb or a one-man arsenal.

About daybreak, when Howden's explosive concoction was ready, the two men carried it in wooden-handled boxes, escorted by Chen Yun and a body of armed Chinese, until they reached Strobridge in the western tunnel. Then, afterward, they traversed the pass to Wesley Bryant's crews on the opposite entrance.

He lost sleep. Forgot to eat. Prowled and growled like a sulky bear at all hours of the day and night. Most of his waking hours were spent secretly observing Wesley Bryant and the men who worked around him. But nothing happened. And so he kept his vigil, talking in monosyllables, eyes straining at each movement, seeing everything that went on under Donner Pass, yet seeing nothing. Finally, on a clear, cold and bright afternoon, a cry rang out of both ends of Summit Tunnel.

"We done it. We broke through!"

Darby, his face covered with a black stubble of beard and his eyes ringed with darkness, merely nodded. Because of his job of being responsible for both tunnels, he'd known better than any of them just when the breakthrough would occur.

Picks hacked into the thin wall separating the two crews and, in moments, each side could see the light beyond and men cried with joy as Darby slumped and watched the frantic celebration. This, too, he'd remember and write of in his novel. It was a historic moment. They'd really done it, beaten the Sierras in spite of unbelievable hardship and ever present danger.

He grinned for the first time in weeks as, in the light of bobbing torches, he saw Strobridge and Crocker hugging Chen Yun and his crew.

Suddenly, Darby realized that something was wrong. Where was Wesley Bryant! Wesley, whom he'd suspected for months. He spun around and. . . .

"Quite an occasion, isn't it?" the cool voice purred.

Darby saw Bryant leaning nonchalantly against the wall, appearing as innocent as a young evangelist at a tent revival.

"You know," he drawled, "I really never thought we'd make it. This is quite a moment."

Darby felt a rush of guilt. Bryant had done everything asked, constructed the Butte Canyon trestle in record time and carried more than his share of the dangerous tunneling this past week under mighty Donner Pass.

The writer was ashamed. "It's your triumph as well," he offered.

"Maybe. But to my way of thinking, until one of our locomotives actually rolls through this tunnel, we haven't really met the terms of our contract."

"It will happen," Darby answered, taken back by the

strange and unexpected comment. What the devil was
with this man? They'd have the final rails laid by tomo.
Strobridge and Crocker would see to that.

He walked away. Bryant offered no comment; he ju
stood there watching the others. To hell with it, Darby
thought. Tomorrow, they *would* meet the terms of the Pacific
Railroad Act.

But tonight? Tonight they'd celebrate.

Wesley Bryant asked for and received permission to
journey down to Auburn with a few men and return by
train in two days. It was his brilliant promotional idea to
telegraph the Sacramento Union and the San Francisco
Chronicle editors and offer them a train ride up to Summit
Tunnel, so that they could record the historic moment when
the mighty Sierras were finally beaten. It was to be an extravagant and symbolic gesture designed for maximum newspaper
exposure. The last rail would be respiked in place, followed
by an elaborate celebration. Finally, the train would roll
through the tunnel and on down to Truckee to meet welcom-
ing Nevada officials.

Even Darby was captured by the drama of the idea and
a little peeved that he'd not thought of it himself.

Sure it was all ceremony, but that was exactly the kind
of publicity they'd need to mollify an already suspicious
Congress that, this time, the Central Pacific Railroad really
had conquered Donner Pass.

"Have everything ready," Bryant advised, "when I return
with those editors. You might. . . ." he faltered, seeming un-
characteristically embarrassed.

"Don't stop," Crocker admonished. "Your idea was
genius. Let's hear the rest."

"Well, with a little effort you could really do it up grand.
Have the last rail polished up and use silver spikes on the
connection."

Crocker frowned. "I don't know," he mused. "We're
trying to squeeze money from Congress. They might think
we're foolish and overly extravagant."

Darby hadn't intended to interrupt, but he did. "I'll pay
for the silver spikes. It will be good publicity for the railroad
as well as my upcoming book."

"Fine!" Crocker beamed, settling the matter quickly.

"One more thing," Bryant said, "put the coolies to work

g up this tunnel. You could have them sweep the
, hang their colored lights, so it appears like a huge
room when I drive in the locomotive. It'll knock the eyes
t of those editors!"

"Now wait just a minute," Strobridge argued loudly.
"This is a train. . . ."

"Oh, Harvey," Crocker said in mild reproof, "we won't
hurt your Summit Tunnel. We're only going to publicize it as
one of the greatest feats in the history of engineering. All the
professional journals will besiege you for interviews."

"Well, they'll have to wait until I'm through whipping
the pants off the Union Pacific."

Crocker winked. "Go to it, Mister Bryant. When you
return, this tunnel under Donner Pass will shine like a
palace."

"Excellent! See you the day after tomorrow."

The spirit of the celebration seized everyone. Charles
Crocker looked positively euphoric as he supervised Chen
Yun and a hundred Chinese preparing for the big moment
when the train of editors and reporters would arrive. The
tunnel was finished and all but a single length of track was
laid and ready. This track was polished until it gleamed as
brightly as the four silver spikes which Darby had insisted on
paying for and which gave him immense pleasure.

After all was cleared, the Chinese hung their bright
lanterns, hundreds of them, close to where tables were placed
across the eastern terminus of track. Somehow, Crocker
managed to have a most excellent punch concocted in their
chemist's kitchen above them on Donner Pass. Finally, the
hour arrived when they heard the long whistle blast of an
approaching train.

"Do you have the speech ready?" Darby asked the
railroad president who kept nervously brushing at his finest
coat.

"Yes, yes. And, as always, Mister Buckingham, you did
a tremendous piece of writing."

Darby bowed, resplendent in his own black suit. Even
the toes of his black, round-toed shoes glistened under the
pretty Chinese lamps hanging twenty feet above the tunnel
floor.

"I'll be glad when all this nonsense is over and we can
get back to work," Strobridge growled. "Did I tell you what

I'm facing at the Little Truckee Bridge just twenty-t...
east of here?"

"No," Crocker snapped peevishly. "And please re...
from informing me *or* the newspapermen about any n...
problems. Remember, as far as we are concerned, hencefort...
the race is on! And now, we are in the driver's seat with the
whip hand. Do I make myself clear?"

Strobridge nodded. Darby could see that their chief of
construction was a hair's breadth away from exploding. He
smiled reassuringly at the man.

"Not much longer, Harvey, then you can return to your
work."

"Good! I hate to waste time with this kind of tomfool-
ery. Yet, I understand the need for a show. That's why I'm
here."

"Excellent, Harvey," Crocker sighed. "Your reward will
be fresh money into the company coffers and the opportunity
to continue your employment. Now, all smiles, because here
comes the train."

It blotted out the circle of sunlight a thousand feet away
at the western portal and seemed to fill Summit Tunnel with
rolling thunder, even though it crawled forward in great
steamy sighs.

"Look at her!" Crocker yelled. "Harvey, she's coming
through Donner Pass one hundred and twenty-four feet under
its surface. What a sight!"

It was a dizzying moment as the locomotive clanked in
towards them, its great smokestack only a couple of feet
below the rocky ceiling.

A violent hiss of steam exploded from behind the wheels
and, with a soft grating of steel, the massive iron beast rolled
to a shuddering halt and sat there, panting.

"Grab the rail!" Crocker ordered. "That's the first thing
I want our editors to see when they disembark."

Darby, Chen Yun and several highly honored Chinese
picked it up, all five hundred pounds of its glistening length.

"Here they come! There's Bryant first and . . ."

No one heard whatever he was going to say next,
because Wesley Bryant jumped onto the clean-swept tunnel
floor, raised his gun and blasted three hanging lanterns to
smithereens.

The chosen Chinese panicked in the boom of confined
gunfire, dropped the polished rail and sprinted east. Darby,

balance, was caught by surprise and, before he
it, the rail was falling into his waist, crushing both
and Chen Yun to the rocky floor. In the split second
e they struck ground, the writer saw Chen Yun try to
ow himself in toward Darby and take more of the weight
nd, in so doing, the man's ribs cracked.

"Freeze!" Bryant screamed through the gunfire. "Strobridge. Crocker. One more from either of you and you're
dead men."

Crocker staggered back in disbelief, knocking one of the
tables over. Gallons of punch and dozens of crystal glasses
shattered to break and spill across the tunnel floor.

"What's going on!" Crocker yelled, righting himself.
"Have you gone mad!"

Darby could scarcely breathe. He was twisted half on
one side, the rail squeezing down high on his chest, making it
nearly impossible to fill his pinched lungs. In all his life—
never—had he experienced such pain.

"What's the matter, Buckingham?" Wesley Bryant asked
solicitously, as he strolled over with four gunmen. "What
happened to all that renowned power when you needed it?"

He leaned over. "What's this? A gold medallion? Why,
that's beautiful. Even more interesting with the bullet mark.
Do you mind if I take it?"

Darby's lips moved but no sound came.

"You must not, then. Thank you. It's much too fine a
work of art to be lost forever in a mountain disaster." He
yanked it viciously, snapping the gold chain.

Darby tried to curse the man, but his voice was a
tortured whisper which made Bryant and his friends laugh,
then turn away to face the railroad president and Strobridge.

"Well, well, you really fixed it up nice," Bryant said,
taking everything in with a sweeping glance. "I kept trying to
imagine how this would all appear when we arrived. It's even
better than I'd expected."

"Where are the newspapermen?" Crocker hissed.

"Who knows? It's my guess they are still waiting in
Auburn. We, ah . . . we had to leave a bit early and I guess we
forgot to notify them of our sudden change of plans. Actually, we never quite got below Cisco because of the Butte
Canyon trestle you let me construct."

Strobridge staggered, "What's. . . ."

"Oh, nothing *yet*," Bryant said. "It's just that I'm sure,

since I didn't mortar in the footings and . . . and, well, . didn't set them in too deeply, that the trestle is er unsafe."

Strobridge leapt for the man's throat and, just as . powerful fingers started to close, one of the gunmen pisto. whipped him to the ground.

"I'll see you hang for this," Crocker vowed, with a murderous vengeance.

"No, you won't," Bryant said lightly. "Because there's about to be a terrible accident in this tunnel. A major catastrophe."

He pointed his gun at the chemist. "You're going to mix one last batch of nitroglycerin, Mister Howden."

The Scottish chemist shook his head violently.

"Take him away!" Bryant ordered. "Do whatever is necessary to change his mind."

Two big men grabbed Howden and he began to struggle until Bryant stepped forward and slapped his face.

"Your wife's name is Emily. You have three small girls and live on Market Street in San Francisco. Second floor. A large building with a neat picket fence and a hardware store underneath."

"How did you . . ."

Bryant slapped him again and the man's head rocked back. "Mix what I ask or your family and that entire building will be gone tomorrow. An explosion, no doubt attributed to be your untended chemicals."

"My God!" Howden shrieked.

"Take him away. And make him hurry."

Darby drifted in and out of unconsciousness. He heard snatches of the conversation and dimly realized what was happening. He willed himself to stay awake, to fight for air and to ease his hands under the rail that threatened to paralyze him and Chen Yun.

By the time the two men returned with a big flask of nitroglycerin and tied both Crocker and Howden up, Darby was able to ease the pressure from his chest. Five hundred pounds. Could he lift it? Hurt and pinned to the rocks? Would he even have a chance or would they shoot him and all the others first?

Bryant was through talking. He'd explained his reasons and almost apologized before he'd had his men grab an unused rail and hammer the final link eastward into place.

.hey stacked the cases of dynamite in a big pile beside
.acks.

"Now for the topping," he proclaimed. Very gingerly, he
.anced the cork-stoppered flask of nitroglycerin on the
.tack of dynamite.

"All aboard," he ordered as his men scrambled onto the
train.

"Well, gentlemen, it's time to go. It really was a splendid
party. Especially the grand finale in which you are about to
participate. Good-bye!"

He lit the fuse to the dynamite, knowing full well it
would provide only part of the force of the blast. The
nitroglycerin would insure the collapse of the entire Summit
Tunnel.

As the locomotive's brakes were released and it rolled
forward down the first few inches of incline, Wesley Bryant
let the engine and tender pass before he swung aboard the
third and only passenger car. Obviously, he intended to travel
fast and light.

That's when Darby began his lift—knowing that he
couldn't fail or they'd all be dead in less than a minute. He'd
always lifted for fun; now he attempted his greatest weight
ever for life itself. His neck sank into his massive shoulders
and a great primordial cry burst from his bloodless lips and
rent the tunnel air.

Arms, big and rock-hard from swinging a hammer and
laying track, knotted and bulged as they drove the rail up,
inch by trembling inch. The blood pounded behind his eyes
and sweat erupted across his quivering body. For a second,
the great arms faltered. He gasped, shouted another tortured
roar and almost passed out as he shoved the rail through the
terrible resistance and up, until it was at arm's reach. Then he
heaved it back over his head to crash against the rock floor
and away from Chen Yun.

Darby staggered up to rip the fuse away. Then he
snatched up the flask of nitroglycerin and, holding it aloft, he
ran after the departing train.

It seemed forever until he was out into the sunlight. The
train was picking up speed now, but he'd closed the gap to
only a dozen yards.

Wesley Bryant shoved his way out onto the rear platform and began firing. The bullets whip-cracked all around,
but the Derby Man was past caring about himself. Half-

blinded by sweat, his eyes redly riveted on the train, he to
one final lunging step, planted his left foot and hurled th
nitroglycerin into a spinning yellow arc.

A bullet grazed his temple and his legs folded as he
pitched headlong between the rails. Then, the earth seemed to
jump and roll and buckle as a brilliant reddish flash shim-
mered high over Donner Pass. The light was hot and it made
Darby turn away and lose his thread of consciousness.

> . . . . *and so, my dear Miss Dolly, we never found a
> trace of any of them, not even of the gold medal-
> lion I so treasured. Mister Crocker has discovered
> an enormous theft of stocks and promissory notes
> —probably the work of that murderous Wesley
> Bryant. I wish I had seen the train explode and him
> with it; I'd rest more assured. Yet, reason tells me no
> ordinary man could have leapt from that passenger
> train and found cover in the perhaps three or four
> seconds it took for the flask of nitroglycerin to
> reach its mark. But Wesley Bryant was no ordinary
> man in any sense of the word. He was the most
> cunning and brilliant villain ever to cross my path.
> Good riddance!*
>
> *In a short time, we'll arrive in Reno, Nevada.
> Please be there, packed and waiting. We have a
> rendezvous with San Francisco while the Central
> Pacific goes on toward its own singular destiny.
> Until we meet again,*
>
> > *Sincerely,*
> > *Darby Buckingham*

AUTHOR'S NOTE

The Central Pacific Railroad's epic struggle to conquer the towering Sierra Nevada Mountains is one of America's finest examples of grit and perseverance overcoming unbelievable odds. There is little argument that the "Big Four"—Collis Huntington, Mark Hopkins, Leland Stanford and the indomitable Charles Crocker—were shrewd businessmen out to make a fortune and grab whatever government funds were available. There is also no question that they were each remarkable men of daring and vision who risked everything to build a railroad that few believed possible. I've presented them as my own perceptions and research have revealed them to me.

That the "Big Four" were convinced a pair of rails could span the Sierras was due, in no small part, to a little-known figure in history by the name of Theodore Judah. He was a brilliant engineer and a bit of a dreamer who first discovered the theoretical route for the Central Pacific. And it was Judah who, with his rolls of survey maps, talked with great zeal of his transcontinental railroad to anyone who would listen—until they *did* listen.

Judah was obsessed with his dream and, eventually, his own enthusiasm and eloquent lobbying in Congress led to the founding of the Central Pacific Rail Road Company. Tragically, Theodore D. Judah died at age thirty-seven of yellow fever while crossing the Isthmus of Panama on his way to New York to obtain additional railroad funding.

Explosion At Donner Pass is a work of fiction based on a great deal of historical fact. The Bloomer Cut was the first great challenge for Harvey Strobridge and I've portrayed him as he really was—hard driving, profane, and the kind of take-charge man who got the job done.

James Harvey Strobridge was a big rawboned man descended from an old New England family. He left home at

143

the age of sixteen to become a tracklayer in 1843 on the Boston and Fitchburg Railroad in Massachusetts and later contracted to build some line for the Naughatuck Railroad in Connecticut. A few years afterward, the California Gold Rush brought him west and, when it ended, he stayed to build the San Francisco and San Jose Railroad. The following year, he joined the Central Pacific and quickly became the person in charge of the entire construction program.

Strobridge was fiercely competitive with his rival railroad out of Nebraska and was proud of the fact that he'd kept the Union Pacific from getting past Promontory, Utah.

He was also responsible for the desperate undertaking to haul locomotives, train cars and steel rails on sleds and rolling logs over Donner Summit. The gamble paid off until Congress discovered they'd leapfrogged the summit tunnels, for the Railroad Act did say that track had to be consecutive. It is also true that, as Superintendent of Construction, Harvey Strobridge's legendary impatience cost him an eye in a black powder explosion.

Charles Crocker probably saw it happen and perhaps it pushed him into using the Chinese, although he had to convince a half-blinded Strobridge by reminding the reluctant construction boss of the Great Wall of China.

Nor did I fabricate the second great obstacle—Cape Horn. Its dimensions are as described and it would have beaten Strobridge except for the fearless Chinese who dangled in their flimsy reed baskets high over the American River.

I invented the sabotage, but there was a Sitka Ice Company, a Panama Steamship Line and several California-Nevada freight and stage lines who hoped the Central Pacific would fail—and when it did not—they did. Also, it is a recorded fact that the westward driving Union Pacific did send a spy to oversee Strobridge and Crocker's progress. The engineer was caught by Crocker and dispatched unharmed but not before he had told the world it would take *at least* three years for Strobridge to blast out the Summit Tunnel.

He was wrong.

After the setback caused by the terms of the Railroad Act, they went back over the pass and worked their hearts out in order to survive. But the other tunnels were as nothing compared to Summit Tunnel and the relentless blizzards they faced in the winters of 1866 and 1867.

If it hadn't been for the decision to hire James Howden

and bring up the inert ingredients for the California-outlawe
nitroglycerin, the Central Pacific might indeed have been there
for three years as their rival's spy had predicted.

In closing, I believe it is important to mention just a
few other historical footnotes. First, President Abraham
Lincoln was responsible for pushing through the Pacific Railroad Act in 1862 and the Central Pacific actually began construction out of Sacramento in January 1863. It took them
nearly five years to beat the Sierras and, during that time, the
Civil War was fought to its conclusion and President Lincoln
was assassinated.

But then the transcontinental race jumped into high gear
and both railroads began to blister their way across the great
plains. It wasn't until May 10, 1869, that Judah's transcontinental railroad was completed.

The Union Pacific Railroad faced some pretty stiff chal-
lenges itself—like plains blizzards, floods and some very
determined Indians. But its Irish tracklayers were equal to the
task—equal enough so that Darby Buckingham would be
interested in telling their side of the story.

First, though, he's got a few other adventures in store,
like a chase north. Farther north than a man like him ever
dreamed. But then, history is about to be made in Sitka,
Alaska.

Historic events. The Derby Man will be a part of them.
Bet on it!

Don't miss the next Derby Man adventure.

NORTH CHASE
by Gary McCarthy

For the Derby Man, it's like reliving a nightmare. Once again he is pitted against his most cruelly dangerous opponent: Wesley Bryant, the brilliant, but utterly evil criminal who almost destroyed the Central Pacific in EXPLOSION AT DONNER PASS.

Bryant lures the Derby Man to San Francisco where he manipulates an underground web of gangsters, using his blood-stained riches to hatch his most ruthless scheme—stealing the vast wealth of Alaska for himself. Vowing to truly stop the twisted genius this time, by killing him with his own hands if necessary, the Derby Man tracks Bryant relentlessly. It is a gruelling chase, leading due north and across the frozen Alaskan tundra, climaxing in the icy savagery of a wilderness blizzard where the Derby Man stands alone in his ultimate battle with a deadly madman!

(*Read the complete Bantam Book, available December 15th wherever paperbacks are sold.*)

Meet The Derby Man— The New Western Powerhouse

Look sharp, hit hard—that's the Derby Man's style. A former circus strongman and hard-knuckle prize winner, he's a fast-moving mountain of muscle who throws himself into the thick of the West's greatest adventures.

THE PONY EXPRESS WAR by Gary McCarthy

The Pony Express—a grueling 2,000 mile race through hell. The pace and terrain are deadly enough but vengeful Paiute warriors and murdering saboteurs led by a sadistic giant threaten to turn the route into a trail of blood. Until one man has the brains and brawn and guts to save the Pony Express—The Derby Man.

SILVER SHOT
by Gary McCarthy

It's hard-rock mining and rock-hard brawling as the Derby Man takes on a boom town. A man could mine fabulous wealth on the Comstock but the Derby Man strikes only a motherlode of trouble when he sets out to expose a spellbinding stock manipulator. His opponent is like a rattle-snake, sabotaging a mine shaft into a pit of death. But with his sledgehammer fists and sharply honed wits, The Derby Man comes roaring back into action.

(Pick up these exciting Derby Man adventures wherever Bantam Books are sold.)

Presenting the exciting opening pages
of a powerful new frontier novel

A KILLER
COMES TO SHILOH
by C. H. Haseloff

Thunder splits the night as the Shiloh death bells
toll the frightening news—a mysterious killer
has brutally cut down three young lives...

The bells that had drawn Joshua Shank into the blackness of the storm were louder now. Hollow and grim came the sound from their iron throats.

In a flash of lightning Joshua saw the church doors with the death notes nailed upon them. Ducking his head against the rain that blew onto the uncovered porch, he climbed the stone steps. Three notes were tacked to the double doors. The torn edges of the papers flapped as fingers of wind slipped beneath and tore them. He held the lantern high, straining to read the words that washed from the wet pages. The window glass beside the door rattled in the wind.

Josh wiped the rain from his eyes. From the Cherokee script, with English below, he read:

"Mary Louise Neil is dead forever. At a murderer's hand. She was a Christian ten years old. Now she has passed from the earth to the place of long rest, leaving behind anguish for the living. Now she has no pain."

The second and third notes were the same except for the names and ages of the children—Jo Belle Walker, age nine; Rebecca Ann Beard, age eight. Josh bent his head, pressing his eyes with his tough brown fingers. Tears mixed with the rain on his cheeks.

"Shank, come inside," Tom Bryan said. "Come out of the weather." Joshua followed him into the church. In the dim light he could see the shoulders of men in the front pews and hear the murmur of their words.

"We don't know it's true," Bob Little said thickly.

"Why would somebody put up something like that on a night like this?" a voice asked from the darkness of a pew.

"What better night for such news?"

"Why didn't whoever put up them notes stay

around? That's purty peculiar puttin' up the notes, ringin' the bell, then disappearin'. Like a joke or somethin'." Pettigrew Wills still wore his house slippers. His nightshirt was stuffed into his britches. The red galluses and striped shirt looked gay and bright in contrast to the dark world. "I was here in five minutes. Somebody done his work and left out the back before I could get here."

"Shank, do you figure it's a joke?" Tom Bryan asked.

"I don't know, Tom. Maybe we ought to check the campmeeting before we go any further."

"That's right. We ought to check," Sam Waters said. "Sure. Somebody ought to go out to the camp. All those girls' families were at the meeting. Saw 'em yesterday evening."

Nobody moved to leave the church for the storm.

"I'll go home and get dressed," said Wills. "And you and me can go out there, Shank."

"By the time you get dressed, Petti, we can all go out there and get back." Sam Waters wanted action. Wills' ways were too slow and ponderous.

"All right. All right. But we'll have to get our horses or a wagon or something. Damn, we're all on foot, and it's three miles out there," Wills said.

"Shank, take my horse," said Tom Bryan. "She's fast, and you're the best rider among us. You can get out there and find the truth before we get organized. Rest of you men go on over to the house. Clary'll have coffee ready by now. We can wait over there together."

Joshua followed Tom around the house and into the stable out back. The barn smelled musty like wet hay. Tom's sorrel mare whinnied at them. Tom Bryan acted as mayor of Shiloh. Like Joshua's family he had settled Shiloh when it was nothing more than some strung out farms along the Indian line. He'd started the first store.

"If it's true, Josh—" he thought a moment. "If it's true, we'll have to keep our heads. Folks'll take it mean. Whoever did it will go to the Nations to hide, probably. We'll wire Fort Smith for a marshall."

"Let's be sure first," Josh said, swinging into the saddle. "I'll be back as soon as I can, Tom." He kicked the mare, ducked the door jam and cantered into the rain.

Tom stood in the doorway a few minutes. He watched the other town men standing on his back porch holding coffee mugs. Clary'd have breakfast soon. "Killin's too good for a bastard who'd kill them children," he heard one of them say. "It'll be a pleasure stringin' him up." It had already begun—the quick, blind call of blood for blood.

A faint light was growing as Joshua rode into the meeting grounds. The camp was three miles from Shiloh and no one on the grounds had heard the bells through the storm. A few men were out driving tent stakes deeper and digging run-off trenches. Smells of bacon and coffee came from the women's area. Men could only enter there from an hour after sun-up until an hour before sundown. That was Reverend Poe's rule. The local preachers bowed to his wisdom. Camp meetings could confuse the feelings of believers. And sexual love might be mistaken for spiritual. So the men and women had separate, inviolate areas to insure high purpose.

The Shiloh campmeeting drew families from Arkansas and Indian country mostly. But every year there was at least a group or two from Missouri or even Iowa or Illinois. They were usually passing through Arkansas on their way to Texas. A lot of folks had felt a need to move on after Appomattox. The border country held too many memories, mostly bad ones and moving on seemed the best way to start fresh. A lot of men had gotten religion in the War, too. In leaving home, they looked for special guidance. And the Shiloh campmeeting had begun as a kind of anointing for those moving West and for those turning back to God.

Every year since the War's end, fewer were Westing, but the hunger for benediction and renewal never slacked. At the end of each summer, people came in their wagons with their families to camp for a week along Sleepy Creek and listen to the preaching and the singing, to find again something that couldn't be dug out of the farm or hung up on the clothes line, to let themselves go in the emotion the meeting brought. Some came in superstitious fear and appeasement of the vengeful force they called "god". And some came because the others were there and ripe for picking.

Reverend Poe's tent sat behind the preaching arbor in the trees. Josh walked the mare down the wide aisle between the log benches of the congregation.

"Preacher," he called out.

The tent flap flew open and the shirtsleeved evangelist offered his tent in a sweeping gesture.

"Get down, brother. It ain't fit to be out." Josh dismounted. "I'm prayin' it'll pass on over before the morning service. There's a lot of sinful souls a needin' salvation. You ain't been around here before, brother, air you?"

"I'm a Friend, Preacher."

"Ain't we all, brother, ain't we all. Set an' eat. Sister Woods just brought me a breakfast that'll bust two bellies."

He sat down and jammed a fork into an egg yolk. The orange-yellow contents oozed onto the plate.

"Love fried eggs. Women is a miracle, brother. To fix a breakfast like this in a drivin' storm."

"Preacher, did you hear the bells?"

"What bells?"

"The Shiloh death bells."

"No, can't says I did." He ran his tongue around his teeth. "You needin' a funeral preached in town? My fee's two dollars."

"We're not sure anyone's dead. The deaths are supposed to be out here in the camp. I've come to see."

"What's that you say?" Preacher Poe stuck a fingernail between his front teeth. "Who's dead out here?"

"The death note said Mary Neil, Jo Belle Walker, and Becka Beard."

The preacher stood up, overturning the table and

dumping the good breakfast onto the dirt. Still holding the fork and wearing his napkin he pushed past Josh and out the front of the tent. He paused a minute then headed around the log pews toward the women's tents. Shank followed, watching the hatless preacher throw down the useless fork and bull through brush and believers.

"They's down here together," he pointed toward a tent set away from the others as he slid standing down the hillside rocks.

By the time he reached the tent, Josh was at his side. They bent together to look inside. Nothing. The tent was empty except for little girl things scattered on the faded quilts—a hair ribbon, a broken comb, a rag doll, a pair of button shoes.

The preacher straightened. "Maybe they's gone to breakfast."

"Look," said Josh dropping to his knees and crawling inside.

He reached back into the corner and grasped a wadded nightdress. The white garment was wet and saturated with a dark substance. He lifted the rear flap over a muddy set of tracks. "They went out through here," he called back over his shoulder.

In the rain outside again, he handed the gown to the preacher. "My God, that's blood," the preacher said, turning the garment in his hands. Blood, pink and fading, ran with the rain through his fingers and onto his boots.

"What's happening?" a short solid woman with a parasol asked the men contemplating the dress. "My God! My God. That's my Mary's dress—"

Preacher Poe threw arms around the woman and held her to him. The disturbance drew others from the women's camp.

"Sister Leona, fetch the men."

Mrs. Neil struggled in his arms to see into the tent. "She ain't there, sister. Don't torment yourself a tryin' to see. What's your name, son?" he suddenly asked Josh.

"Joshua Shank."

The preacher's eyes glazed over with a biblical ecstasy. "They're over yonder across the Jordan, brother Joshua. Gird up the fighting men and lead them into the land of our enemy. Smite them. Smite them hip and thigh. Blood for blood. Eye for eye. Tooth for tooth. Kill the Amalekites, Joshua."

By this time, men were sliding down the slope to join the crowd gathering in the rain. "Look," shouted a boy pointing across the creek into the brush. Rain had washed the mud from something beneath the blackberry bushes. "It's a foot." The crowd surged toward the creek bank.

"Stop. Stop where you stand!" shouted Shank. "If you all crush about now, you'll ruin any clues the rain hasn't. You men, take your wives to their tents. The preacher'll tell you who's missing."

In the crowd Josh saw faces of men he knew. "Whiting, Trimble, LeFevre, come with me. Boy," he said to a youngster pulling up the tent flap, "my horse is at the preacher's tent. Ride to town. Tell Tom Bryan, 'It's true. Send for a marshall.' Then bring him back here. Don't talk to anybody else. Do you understand?" The boy nodded and ran up the hill.

"Trimble, get some help and try to keep people off this stuff around the tent. Whiting, LeFevre, let's see what's over there."

Joshua and his men waded into Sleepy Creek. Looking over his shoulder, he saw Trimble and another man guarding the tent. The preacher, still holding Mrs. Neil, was making his way up the rocky slope with the crowd behind him.

"Funny ain't it," said LeFevre. "Half hour ago folks couldn't think of anything but stayin' dry. Now they're walkin' around in the rain, and they don't even care."

There was no further talk as the three men walked up the muddy slope to where the foot had been seen. The body in the brush was that of a girl child, small and pale. The throat was cut out.

"Oh God," Whiting grabbed his mouth, walked a few feet away and leaned against a tree.

"Can you tell who it is, Josh?" asked LeFevre shifting the tobacco from his cheek.

"Jo Belle . . ." The words caught in Shank's throat. He cleared it. "It's Jo Belle Walker."

There is an evil killer loose in Shiloh. Quickly the terrified drive for revenge threatens to destroy not only the town but the nearby peaceful Cherokee nation. Although he is a Quaker, Joshua Shank is the only man strong enough to see the killer brought to justice without more blood being shed. Until suddenly the killer forces the man of peace into a death-stalk—the most savage encounter of Shank's entire life.

(Read the complete Bantam Book, A KILLER COMES TO SHILOH, by C. H. Haseloff, available June 15th wherever paperbacks are sold.)

Great stories of the Lone Star frontier

Elmer Kelton's
TALES OF

TEXAS

Elmer Kelton is one of the great storytellers of the American West with a special talent for capturing the fiercely independent spirit of his native Texas. Now, for the first time, Bantam Books has collected many of Elmer Kelton's exciting Western novels in a series, TALES OF TEXAS, to be published on a regular basis beginning in July, 1981.

Each of the TALES OF TEXAS is dramatically set in the authentic Texas past. These stories filled with the special courage and conflicts of the strong men and women who challenged a raw and mighty wilderness and fought to build a frontier legend —Texas.

CAPTAIN'S RANGERS
(Available August 15th 1981)

The Nueces Strip—a stretch of coastal prairie and desert wasteland lying between the two rivers that bordered Texas and Mexico. Long after the Mexican War this parched land remained a war zone, seared by hatred on both sides and torn by lawless raids of looting and burning. By the Spring of 1875 the Strip was ready to explode—for this was the year Captain McNelly and his Rangers were sent down from the North. Their mission— "clean up the Nueces Strip."

MASSACRE AT GOLIAD

(*Available September 15th 1981*)

In 1834 Thomas and Josh Bucalew came to the rugged new country that was Texas. The land that was soon to be ravaged by the battle of the Alamo, at the brutal massacre at Goliad and its bloody sequel, San Jacinto. Because of Thomas' hatred of Mexicans they separated, but the two brothers were re-united when the smoldering violence exploded into savage war.

(*Don't miss Elmer Kelton's TALES OF TEXAS, available wherever Bantam Books are sold.*)

"REACH FOR THE SKY!"

and you still won't find more excitement or more thrills than you get in Bantam's slam-bang, action-packed westerns! Here's a roundup of fast-reading stories by some of America's greatest western writers:

BANTAM'S #1
ALL-TIME BESTSELLING AUTHOR
AMERICA'S FAVORITE WESTERN WRITER

☐	14931	THE STRONG SHALL LIVE	$2.25
☐	14977	BENDIGO SHAFTER	$2.50
☐	13881	THE KEY-LOCK MAN	$1.95
☐	13719	RADIGAN	$1.95
☐	13609	WAR PARTY	$1.95
☐	13882	KIOWA TRAIL	$1.95
☐	13683	THE BURNING HILLS	$1.95
☐	14762	SHALAKO	$2.25
☐	14881	KILRONE	$2.25
☐	20139	THE RIDER OF LOST CREEK	$2.25
☐	13798	CALLAGHEN	$1.95
☐	20180	THE QUICK AND THE DEAD	$2.25
☐	14219	OVER ON THE DRY SIDE	$1.95
☐	13722	DOWN THE LONG HILLS	$1.95
☐	20219	WESTWARD THE TIDE	$2.25
☐	14227	KID RODELO	$1.95
☐	14104	BROKEN GUN	$1.95
☐	13898	WHERE THE LONG GRASS BLOWS	$1.95
☐	14411	HOW THE WEST WAS WON	$1.95

Buy them at your local bookstore or use this handy coupon for ordering:

BANTAM'S #1
ALL-TIME BESTSELLING AUTHOR
AMERICA'S FAVORITE WESTERN WRITER

THE SACKETTS

Meet the Sacketts—from the Tennessee mountains they headed west to ride the trails, pan the gold, work the ranches and make the laws. Here in these action-packed stories is the incredible saga of the Sacketts —who stood together in the face of trouble as one unbeatable fighting family.

Bantam Book Catalog

Here's your up-to-the-minute listing of over 1,400 titles by your favorite authors.

This illustrated, large format catalog gives a description of each title. For your convenience, it is divided into categories in fiction and non-fiction—gothics, science fiction, westerns, mysteries, cookbooks, mysticism and occult, biographies, history, family living, health, psychology, art.

So don't delay—take advantage of this special opportunity to increase your reading pleasure.

Just send us your name and address and 50¢ (to help defray postage and handling costs).